ISBN: 978-1-77409-119-7

SEAWEED

A MERFOLK TALE

LEE STRAUSS

MORE YA BOOKS BY LEE STRAUSS

Buy on Amazon or read FREE with Kindle Unlimited!
Clockwise

ClockwiseR
Like Clockwork
Counter Clockwise
Clockwork Crazy
Clocked

Seaweed

Love, Tink (episode 1)
New York, New York (episode 2)
Love Stinks (episode 3)
Peter Panelli (episode 4)
Dazed & Befuddled (episode 5)
Fairy Madness (episode 6)

Love, Tink (the complete series)

*H*e stood at the bonfire with his head high, shoulders back, radiating a military type of confidence. With one hand he swept his dark hair across his forehead and even through the flickering orange hue I could tell he had amazing eyes.

Something drew his gaze to mine. Fate? Providence? My heart stopped beating. He smiled shyly then glanced away, his focus returning to the erratic dancing of the flames.

I'd never seen him before which, in Eastcove New Brunswick, was an unusual occurrence.

My best friends, Samara and Becca, stood beside me, each with a can of Coke in their hands.

"Who is that?" Samara shouted over the noise of the music blaring from a truck that was backed up close to the pit. Four teens sat squeezed together on the tailgate laughing at someone's joke.

Becca shouted back, "I think it's a *new* guy."

Samara fiddled with her long black braid. "Since when does anyone new move to Eastcove?"

Good question.

"He's cute!" Becca said.

"I saw him first." I gave him a little finger wave and started to make my way to the other side of the fire. I meant to clearly establish my intentions to claim this new boy.

I was intercepted by Colby Johnston.

"Hey, Seaweed." He moved in a little too close for comfort. I took a subtle step sideways.

"Hi."

I couldn't stop twisting my neck, watching the mysterious new guy. Another girl was chatting him up and a tickle of irritation curled up in my gut.

"What're you looking at?" Colby's gaze followed mine. "Ah, him."

I couldn't believe I hadn't heard about *him* already. East-cove was a dying fishing village, the kind of town people *left*. A new family would've definitely made the gossip hotline.

"So, about us?" Colby said, like he'd said it a thousand times. Which he had.

I took a sip from my water bottle and tried to pretend I didn't hear him.

"Dori. We need to talk about this."

I let out a frustrated sigh. "Okay, talk."

He swigged back his drink, then spoke into my ear, "I know you already know this, but I guess I always thought we'd get together sometime. Sometime soon."

I did know this. I think everybody knew this. We were swim team champions. We were good friends. Even Samara and Becca thought we'd make the perfect couple.

Colby's dark eyes reflected the jumping flames, and I resisted the urge to reach over and rub his buzz cut, wanting to make everything okay.

Instead, I shook my head softly. "I'm sorry." I hated hurting him. I couldn't help that I didn't feel the same way.

His head fell forward. "I know, Seaweed. Forget I said anything." He slipped away, losing himself in the crowd. I blew out a heavy sigh.

The flames of the bonfire licked high toward the murky, open sky. The burning wood snapped and popped at its base. Smoke meshed with the salty essence of the sea and I breathed it in slowly. Peering through the sparks I kept my focus on the mystery guy. He caught me looking at him and this time he didn't look away. We gradually moved toward each other, until finally we were side by side.

"Hey."

"I'm Dori Seward," I said, loudly.

"Dori?"

"Yeah, like the fish in the movie." Did I really just say that? "It's a nickname because I like to swim. A lot." Okay, so much for smooth. Just kill me now.

He motioned for us to move away from the music toward the waves slapping the shore.

"It's a little quieter over here," he said. Then he shook my hand. "I'm Tor Riley." It was warm and strong.

"Where did you move from?" I asked, tucking my hands back into my pockets.

"Maine."

"So, you're not that far from home."

"I guess. I still have the Bay of Fundy."

He sipped his soda and I relieved my dry throat with my water.

"What do you think of Eastcove so far?"

He shrugged. "It's okay."

"What brought your parents here?" I knew there wasn't much left for work.

Tor fussed at the sand with his shoe. "Uh, I'm not here with them. They, uh, travel a lot. I'm living with my uncle."

I got the impression it was a touchy subject.

"What about you?" he said, turning the tables. "Tell me about you."

We headed back toward the warmth of the bonfire as I gave him the rundown of my average family—a mom, a dad, two brothers. I was about to broach the less than exciting topic of pets when I was interrupted by shouting and loud laughter on the other side of the fire pit. Sawyer shook his can and let the contents fly. Mike got him back with his drink, and before long everyone was in on it.

I looked at Tor and he smirked. That was when I did the stupidest thing ever. I opened my water bottle and swung it at Tor, splashing him right in the face.

I thought it would be funny. It was all in the name of fun and games. But instead of laughing and throwing his soda back at me, he looked at me with wide, horror-filled eyes.

Next thing I knew, Tor was sprinting down the beach into the darkness.

"Tor!" I yelled. With all the shouting, the blaring music, and the roar of waves crashing to shore, no one heard me.

"Tor!" I took off after him, and in the mayhem, no one noticed. "I'm sorry. Please, come back."

I could make out his outline in the moonlit darkness when I followed him around the bend. My heart raced and I wanted to tackle him to the ground until he told me what was going on.

I didn't have a chance. I got to a cropping of rocks just in time to see him dive into the frigid ocean.

2

———

*T*here was a quarter moon out, but a haze of clouds had drifted by. I couldn't see Tor anywhere. I raced along the beach scanning the dark waters, desperate to see his head bob up and for him to swim back to shore. And when he did, I was going to kill him. New guy or not.

Nothing.

"Tor!" I shouted again. My heart beat madly against my ribs. Before I could think it through rationally, all those years of lifeguard training kicked into gear. I stripped off my hoodie, threw off my shoes and dove in.

It was freaking cold! The North Atlantic was not famous for its warm waters, even in June. Especially at night. I decided then and there that this guy Tor was completely crazy. A lunatic. Nut house candidate.

Even so, I couldn't let him drown.

I swam out as far as I dared, icy waves slapping my face, causing my breath to catch. I searched above the surface and below: Where are you, Tor? Please, surface, surface.

Only dark, rolling waves. No sign of him. My core was

dangerously cold, hypothermia a real danger. I had no choice but to go back.

My fingers wouldn't work. They were frozen, locked in a cramped position. I was shivering so hard, my bones rattled. I struggled to get my clothes on, freaking because it was taking so long and I needed to get back to the bonfire, pronto. Somehow I managed to slip my feet into my sneakers, but I didn't bother attempting the laces.

I limped back to the bonfire and tugged on Samara's sleeve.

"Dori!" Samara cried out when she saw the condition I was in. "What happened to you?"

I pushed close to the fire for warmth.

"It's T-t-or," I stammered. My teeth were chattering.

"That new guy?"

"Y-yes."

"What happened? Did he push you in?"

"N-no. He, uh, fell into the ocean and didn't come out." I don't know why I lied for him, but diving in was just too stupid.

"What?"

"I tried to find him, but I couldn't see."

"Oh, my God." Samara jumped to action. "Dori needs a blanket, she's wet and freezing."

"What's going on?" Mike shouted.

"It's that new guy. He fell into the ocean. Dori saw it. He didn't come back out."

Colby took charge after that. He instructed groups of three or four to scour the beach.

I was as close to the fire as I could stand without burning the car blanket that was wrapped tightly around my shoulders.

Colby approached me. "Are you okay?"

He knew me. He knew I could handle cold water and the stress that came with lifeguarding, but he was asking a deeper question.

"I don't know."

He considered my answer, then added, "We should go to the police."

OFFICER BOB RICHTER took our story seriously and immediately dispatched a search and rescue team. I was warmer now but still, I couldn't stop quivering. Nerves. Fear. Did I just watch someone dive to his death? I felt a sob build in my chest.

Strong, sturdy arms wrapped around my shoulders and I knew it was Colby. I tilted my head to see his face. His mouth was set in a grim line, and I could tell by the dark narrow squint of his eyes that he was worried about me. Tor too, but mostly me. His arms felt good and not just because they warmed me up. I pressed into him and he didn't let go.

Maybe I was wrong about Colby. At least I knew who he was. I knew his family. I knew where he lived and what his bedroom looked like (a mess). I knew his favorite food (steak and shrimp kabobs) and his favorite movies (*Star Wars*, the old ones).

I didn't know anything about Tor and I'd risked my life for him tonight. I couldn't understand what had happened at all. Why he ran and why he dove into the ocean.

I really hoped they found him.

Mom and Dad were snuggling on the couch watching a movie and Mom jumped up when she saw Colby and me walk in.

"Dori, what happened?"

Though the shivering had subsided somewhat, my hair was still a wet matted mess and I suspected my lips were an unhealthy shade of blue.

Colby answered for me. "A new kid from our school fell into the ocean and didn't come out. Dori tried to rescue him."

"Oh, my goodness," Mom said, reaching for me. "Let's get you upstairs and into a hot shower."

Dad and Colby waited in the living room.

"He fell in?" Mom said as she guided me up the stairs. "How did that happen?"

I didn't want to tell her the truth—that Tor dove in of his own accord. My teeth chattered whenever I opened my mouth, keeping me from saying anything coherent anyway. Mom ran the water, until steam formed. "Okay, get in. We'll be waiting for you downstairs."

I stood naked under the spray, the blast of heat cloaking my head like a sheet. I turned and let it wash my face and then my back, until my core warmed up fully. I ran the hot water tank dry.

I dressed in extra layers and blow-dried my hair. I knew Mom would be expecting me to be wearing my pajamas when she saw me, ready to hop right into bed, but I was determined to go out to look for Tor some more.

"Dori?" Mom's eyebrows arched when she spotted me fully clothed descending the stairs.

"I'm fine now, Mom. Totally warm. No harm done."

"You're not going out again," she said. "You've suffered quite a shock to your system. Enough's enough."

"I agree with your mother," Dad said. "They'll find him. The Coast Guard is trained for this kind of thing. You don't want to get in the way."

A thread of panic weaved through me and I was afraid they were really going to keep me from going out again.

"I'll be with her," Colby said. "I'll make sure she gets home safely."

I tossed him a look that said *Thank you.*

"I won't get in the way, Dad. I know better than that, but I can't just sit here."

Colby shifted uncomfortably from leg to leg, not wanting to be a part of a family argument, but I was betting his presence would get me my way. Mom didn't like to cause a scene in front of company.

"Mom, we're just going to go back to the beach, see if anything has happened. I won't be out long, I promise."

Mom sighed and gave in. "Okay, but be home by eleven."

I grabbed a warmer jacket and then Colby's arm. "Let's go."

"You're sure you want to do this?" Colby said as we walked down Main Street toward the beach.

"Yeah, I'm sure. I just have to know."

"You did everything you could, you know? Even though it was crazy for you to dive into the bay after dark. You're a good swimmer, but no one's immune to the force of the current, especially when disoriented by darkness. You know this."

My chest tightened. "You're not exactly making me feel better."

"I don't know if it's possible to survive what happened to Tor or not, but something terrible could've happened to you." His eyes settled on mine. "You scared me."

I didn't know what to say to that. He was right about the risks, and it was nice to know that he cared about what happened to me. I was sorry that I'd scared him.

We walked the rest of the way in silence. A small gathering of teens remained at the bonfire. The truck with the music was gone leaving just the sounds of the waves and wind to tease us.

"Sorry, man," Sawyer said when he saw us. "No sign of him anywhere, up or down the beach."

He looked kindly at me. "You okay?"

I nodded, then gazed out over the ocean. A searchlight from the Coast Guard vessel flickered past along the shoreline. I followed the lighted path with my eyes. Nothing but soft foamy waves lapped the beach.

I couldn't help myself. I let out a big sobby hiccup.

"Dori?" Samara called. She and Becca were beside me in an instant, Becca with a tissue she'd just whipped out of her pocket. "We didn't see you come back."

"Thanks." I accepted the tissue and made good use of it. "I'm fine, now."

We waited around the fire, with only the sound of quiet murmurs as the number of teens continued to peter out. The fire had shrunk to embers, and Mike and Sawyer collected pails of water to extinguish it fully.

I didn't know where the time went, but it was almost eleven already. Colby offered to walk me back.

"Let's stop at the police station one more time," I said.

"You don't want to be late for your curfew, Dori."

"We won't. Just a quick check."

When we walked in, an elderly man was at the counter, speaking to Officer Bob.

"I'm very sorry that Tor has caused this concern," he said with a deep, baritone voice. "I assure you he is fine."

I grabbed the man's arm, startling him. "Are you Tor's uncle?"

I knew he was before he said a word. From a distance he looked like any number of old, weathered fishermen I'd seen all my life, with greasy gray hair and a rugged demeanor, but up close I could see the difference. His skin was smooth with far fewer wrinkles than you would expect, and his hair was practically glossy. His posture was straight and broad shouldered. You could see that he had that old man strength about him, no sign of elderly frailty in the least.

"And you must be Dori," he said, an amused smile spreading across his face.

"What happened to him? Why did he..." I remembered

Colby was standing behind me at that moment and I didn't want to divulge that Tor had gone into the ocean on purpose.

"It was an accident, my dear. He never meant to scare anyone, and you can rest assured that he is safe and sound."

In an instant my relief turned to anger. It was no accident—that I was certain of. Tor was safe and sound until I saw him again. Then he was dead meat.

3

I folded myself into the back seat of the Rotten Apple —aka the red '87 Tercel my brother Luke had bought for five hundred bucks. Mom made Luke drive me to Saint John for swim club now that he had his license.

I took the backseat, even though I had to squish to fit in, because in two short minutes, Luke's girlfriend of one month, Jolene, would claim the passenger seat.

We pulled into Jolene's yard, the Rotten Apple rattling and puffing smoke as we idled, and Luke honked the horn. Jolene bounded out the front door and greeted us both with a very cheerful hello. She leaned over to Luke, and I looked away discreetly as they locked lips.

"Hey," I said, not wanting to be rude. She only came along so that Luke had someone to hang out with while he burned an hour and a half waiting for me in Saint John. It wasn't that I didn't like Jolene. It was just that when she came, I had to sit in the backseat with Colby. I worried about all the mixed signals I'd sent to him the night before, accepting his warmth and comfort.

Like we were a couple and not just friends.

Colby was waiting on his front porch when we pulled onto his gravel driveway, a cloud of dust announcing our arrival. He pushed off the steps, throwing his swim gear over his shoulders. He had an athletic build, his T-shirt tight around well-formed biceps. He had soft facial features and dark-as-night eyes. I could see why a lot of girls liked him.

"Hi," I said when he pushed himself in.

"You okay?" he said, not taking his eyes off mine.

"Yeah, I'm fine." I reached over to rub his buzz cut, a ritual I'd done a million times over the years. I loved the soft bristly feeling on my palm and the shape of his head.

Then an image flashed through my mind, unbidden—my fingers running through Tor's dark wavy hair. Thinking of him caused tiny little flares to shoot through my body. I pinched my eyes closed and shook it off. He was a freak. Not worth my time.

It took thirty minutes traveling north on Highway 1 to get to Saint John. We followed the coastline along the rocky beaches and inlets, whitecaps crashing against black, jagged edges.

Jolene turned the radio on to an Indies station, and Colby and Luke started in on dirt biking stats, Colby's second passion after swimming.

Finally, we got to the Canada Games Aquatic Center, aka, *Centre Aquatique Jeux du Canada*, on the corner of Union and Market. Some people complained about the strong chlorine smell, but I loved it. Almost as much as the salty scent of the ocean. I walked through the marked doors and took a deep breath. Ah, my second home.

I blocked out the chatter that echoed through the change rooms, suiting up in a plain red, one-piece Speedo, and stuffed my waist long white-blond hair into an ugly swim cap. Yes, it would be easier if I'd just cut my hair, but my hair was my trademark. It was the envy of all the girls at Eastcove Secondary School, apparently, with the exception of Samara. She was First Nations Canadian, and with her high cheekbones and chocolate caramel eyes, she had a Pocahontas thing going that would not only make John Smith look twice, but every guy on the planet.

"Listen up," Coach said once we did a round of warm up laps and gathered at one end. "The Junior Nationals are in Vancouver this summer. As you know, there's room for three of you on the team. From now on I'm keeping track of times and technique. I'll let you know who makes it at the end of June."

I looked at Colby whose dark eyes were staring hard back at me. We both knew we'd make the top two. But who would be number one?

Coach ordered us out of the water and into position. I replaced my goggles, nailing the wet alien look, wrapped my toes over the edge of the pool and squatted. Coach blew the whistle and we dove. My lane was next to Colby's so we could gauge each other's progress. I knew Coach did that on purpose because we were both competitive people and he wanted to use that to spur us on.

I felt my heart race, aware of Colby's form beside mine just one stroke ahead. I stopped taking a breath every stroke, trying to make up time, wanting to catch him. I felt myself gaining. He hit the wall just before I did, flipped and headed back down the fifty-meter long lane. I was right on his heels, focused and in rhythm. *Stroke, stroke, stroke.* I was catching Colby. I sensed it before I saw it. I could beat him.

But then I held back. I always held back. I let him win.

"Dori," Coach said as I toweled off after practice. His eyes darted sideways a few times before settling on me. Uh oh. Coach probably wondered how Colby and I almost hit the same time, since Colby was obviously bigger and stronger. I wondered that myself. Did he think I cheated? Or worse, did he think I took drugs or something?

A heavy thug settled in my stomach. "Yeah, Coach?"

"I watched you during that first race."

"I didn't win," I said. "Colby did."

"I know. You didn't win, Dori, but you didn't breathe either."

I felt my eyelids flutter. "What?"

Coach cocked his head. "The whole second length. You didn't bring your head up to breathe once."

"I didn't? I must've. Coach, you weren't watching me the whole time."

"Yes, I was."

What was the matter with me? I didn't take a breath? Not once? I was so focused on beating Colby and then not beating him, I didn't even notice.

Coach fiddled with the papers on his clipboard. "You have an extraordinary ability to hold your breath. That's extremely useful to you as a swimmer."

More eyelid fluttering. "Uh, thanks?"

He went back to his office, and I left for the change rooms feeling relieved. So, I could hold my breath for a long time. So what? There were probably lots of people who could do that, like there were people with really long tongues who could touch their noses or people who were double jointed and could twist themselves into a pretzel. It was just like that. A freaky gift.

When I looked up, I saw Ally gawking at me. She'd been on the swim team as long as I had, but never placed near the top three. I wondered if she was staring because she'd noticed my freaky gift. But then I realized she was staring at my legs.

I glanced down. They were beet red.

"Dori," Ally finally said. "What's wrong with your legs?"

Now that I'd noticed the rash, suddenly they were unbelievably itchy. "I don't know. Maybe the chlorine is out of whack."

"My legs are okay."

I checked them out. She was right. There was nothing wrong with her legs. Mine were itching and scaling like crazy.

"That looks like eczema," Ally said. "A really bad case of eczema."

Great. Just great. Not only did I have a circus worthy weirdo gift, I looked like a gigantic lobster, too.

4

ark, Luke and Dad were already seated at the
table for Sunday brunch. With all five of us
plus Nana who'd popped in, too, it was a tight fit. We'd become
experts at keeping our elbows in and dodging tall beverage
glasses.

Tor's escape on Friday night was the talk around the table.

"Dori," Nana said with a worried frown, "I heard you tried
to save him. In the dark!"

One thing about a town like Eastcove, everyone knew
everybody's business.

"It was no big deal, Nana. I'm trained for that kind of thing.
Besides, I didn't find him. He found his own way out."

"Must be some kind of swimmer," Dad said. He was a
gentle giant, beefy with wide shoulders and warm, soft brown
eyes.

"Or some kind of stupid," Luke quipped, as he spooned
applesauce onto his fish pancakes.

"Shut up!" I said, scowling.

"Apparently he fell," Mark said, showing some pity. "It

happens."

"Yeah, Luke," I said defensively, "it happens."

"I'm just glad everyone is okay." Mom stood scanning the table for anything missing and then grabbed the salt, pepper and nutmeg out of the cupboard.

Nana eyeballed me as she chewed. She was slim from working in her flower garden, and from walking everywhere. She didn't believe in cars, and if she needed to go to "the city," Mom would take her. Her soft skin folded around a face accustomed to smiling and her short gray curly hair still had signs of the same blond Mom and I shared.

She put her fork down, reached across Mom's lap, grabbed my hand and squeezed. "You really should stay out of the ocean, Dori."

The way she said it kind of freaked me out, all earnest and foreboding-like. I wondered if maybe Nana was starting to lose some of her marbles. She was getting kind of ancient. I gave her a reassuring smile.

"I'll be fine, Nana."

I spent the rest of the afternoon studying for exams. My cat Crosby lounged on my bed, his amber eyes languidly following my movements with mild curiosity.

"Hey, Crosby." I couldn't resist running my fingers through his fur. I pressed my face into his forehead. Ah, fuzz therapy.

By Monday I was almost forgiving Tor, and I found myself looking for him at school, in the yard and in the halls, but he was a no show. Just as well. Everyone was buzzing about how the new guy, Tor Riley, had fallen into the ocean.

Only I knew the truth.

The day was a blur of exams and I wondered if Tor was about to fail grade ten. Or did it matter, since he was starting school two weeks before it ended, which was weird if you thought about it. Maybe he just wanted to make friends.

I told myself not to think about him, but still I thought about him. What was the matter with me?

Luke dropped me home after school before he headed to work at Joe's Garage. Mom had left a note saying she had taken Nana shopping so I was alone in the house with Sidney, our golden lab, and Crosby. I took turns scratching behind their ears as I snacked on milk and cookies.

I wasn't often home alone, and it felt strange. I'd never noticed how loud the fridge motor was before, or how the kitchen clock had a soft tick.

I almost turned on the TV for company when I heard a knock at the door. I waited, but no one opened it with an accompanying "hello." That was the usual unspoken arrangement in this town.

Sidney beat me to the door and started barking. I turned the knob and opened it.

Tor.

My jaw dropped in surprise and then promptly clamped.

"What do you want?"

"I want to explain what happened the other night."

"Oh, the night when you ran away from me and dove into the ocean and never resurfaced? That night?"

He looked me straight in the eye. "Yeah, that night."

I shook my head. I wasn't even sure I wanted to know anymore.

Tor leveled his deep greens on me and I was suddenly curious. What could he possibly say?

I relented and was about to ask him to come in, but Sidney was squirming like mad and I wasn't sure how long I had before Mom got home. I grabbed my jacket. "Let's walk."

We automatically ended up at the beach, and continued padding through the rough sand until we came to a grouping of ragged black rocks. Tor climbed up on an enormous one and I followed, making sure there was a good distance between us. The wind whipped my loose hair against my face. Sidney settled in on the beach beside us.

Seagulls soared and squawked overhead. Crabs crept across the sand then dug and buried themselves in safe little holes. The tide in the Bay of Fundy was rising and out on the horizon I saw a blast of water shoot into the sky.

"Did you see that?" Tor said.

"Yeah. Probably a humpback."

We waited and it jumped—its heavy gray pleated body defying gravity and crashing back into the sea.

"Wow," I said. "It doesn't matter how many times I see something like that, I'm always blown away. It's so amazing."

"Yeah, she's amazing."

I looked at him. "How do you know it's a she?"

"Oh, I don't know," he said quickly. "Just a guess."

I let the salty air massage my face and took a deep breath. The air revived me and calmed me at the same time. I was soothed by the rhythmic music of the waves, and found it hard to keep my anger level up.

"Dori, I'm sorry about the other night."

I stared at him. His face was kind and gentle, but his eyes were sad.

"I don't understand what happened. I know I shouldn't have thrown my water at you, but I was just trying to have fun. I didn't mean anything by it."

"I know, and I wasn't mad about that. I can't explain why I had to run. I'm just hoping that you can accept my apology."

Looking away, I mouthed, "You frightened me." I didn't think he would hear me, but he did.

"I know. And for that I'm truly sorry."

"But you dove into the water and it was absolutely freezing cold. I went in after you."

"I know you did. I wish you hadn't and I'm really glad you're okay."

"So, tell me why you did it. Why did you dive in? What happened to you?"

Tor sighed heavily and searched the beach with his eyes, as if the answer would peek out like a turtle's head.

"I can't tell you. I'm sorry."

"Fine." I climbed off the rock and stormed away. Tor jumped down, running after me, and grabbed my arm.

"Please, Dori. Don't be mad. I'm really sorry and I want to be friends."

"You want to be friends?" I shook my head. I didn't know if I could do *friends* with this guy. Despite my anger, I still found him incredibly cute and alluring. I surprised myself by thinking that I might want more than friends.

"Me, too."

Me too, what? Did he just read my mind? "Excuse me?"

"I mean, yes, I want to be friends. And maybe more, someday. When you're no longer angry with me."

I felt breathless, kind of faint. I dropped to my butt on the sand.

"You want to be more than friends?" I squeaked out. "Someday?"

Tor grinned crookedly and nodded.

Wow, I hadn't seen this coming. This mysterious boy had a lot of secrets, but maybe there really was a reason he couldn't tell me them right now. He was like a present wrapped in a big bow, waiting to be opened. I didn't know all of Tor's favorite things or what he looked like in preschool, where he grew up or what his family was like. But the discovery could be exciting. Anticipation was half the fun.

There was something different about Tor Riley, and I liked that.

5

I opened my locker and grabbed my books for the last class before lunch. Earth science.

Part way down the hall, I ran into Tor exiting Mr. Grimer's history class. He moved with a movie star quality that made my knees feel like elastic bands. Of course, I never for one moment forgot that Tor had said he wanted to be more than friends one day. For some reason, this thought made me overjoyed.

"Hi!" I said, realizing belatedly that I sounded way too enthusiastic. I tried to calm my voice down. "How was history?"

"Fine," Tor said with a very pleasant smile. "I like to know what went on in the world before now. Helps to figure out what's going to happen next."

Wow, deep. "Yeah, I like that, too. So, what's your next class?"

He paused to check his schedule. "Earth science."

Yes! Finally a class we had together. But I kept it cool. "Oh, I have Earth science, too, so we're in the same class." Our school was so small there was only one class for each subject per grade.

Tor nodded. "Lead the way."

I was almost giddy walking down the hall, side by side with Tor. All the girls glanced at me with envy. Tor was new. He survived an ocean mishap. He was mysterious.

This was what it would be like to be a couple. Yes, Tor and Dori, the cutest couple at Eastcove. Sounded good to me.

Tor smelled terrific, too, musky and fresh, like he'd slept in the forest. I was so pre-occupied with him, I almost missed the door to the class.

"Oh, here. This is it." I stumbled over his feet as we back-tracked a couple steps, grabbing onto his arm to keep from face-planting.

"Oh, sorry." I flushed with embarrassment and something else that had to do with the fact that I was hanging on to his arm.

"No, problem." A grin tugged on his lips as he set me aright.

Once inside the classroom, I wasn't sure what to do. I made a quick calculation. I wanted to sit beside Tor, but that would've meant changing seats from my usual spot, something everyone, including Mr. Teaworthy, would've noticed and mocked. I moved slowly to my desk, still undecided when Mr. Teaworthy spoke.

"You must be Tor Riley," he said, his belly jiggling with the effort. "Just in time for the end of the year and final exams. There's an empty chair at the back."

Great, just great. Not only could I not sit with Tor, I couldn't see him either, since he was behind me in the same row. Everyone would notice if I tried to steal glances at him.

To make matters infinitely worse, Tiffany MacMillan sat right across the aisle from him. I had time to see her flick her chocolate (crap) colored hair, bat her (fake) eyelashes and spring her starlet (horsy) smile on him before Mr. Teaworthy called us to order.

My body stiffened with frustration. I felt my jaw tighten as I ground my teeth.

Mike and Sawyer took their seats on either side of me. Mike looked at Tor and Tiffany and shook his head. "Sorry, Dori," he said, laughing. I stuck my tongue out at him.

"Class, today I'm showing a video on the Pacific Garbage Patch. Then you will write a five hundred-word essay on what you learned and how you feel about the social responsibility citizens of planet Earth have toward it. Sawyer, you can kill the lights."

We watched as a blob of plastic and garbage twice the size of Texas bobbed about in the Pacific Ocean. The narrator went on about how pollution was endangering sea life and bird life and basically every other kind of life.

I glanced back at Tor when the bell rang. He stared out the window, and his face flashed with emotion. Anger? Sadness? Who wouldn't be ticked off by a video like that? We were screwing up our planet.

Tiffany scooped her arm through his before I had a chance to make it to the back of the room.

Whatever. I left them and went straight to my locker where I plucked out my bag lunch. Then I headed for the vending machines.

And bought dulse. Two bags. Dulse was dried edible seaweed grown in the Bay of Fundy. And yes, they sold it at our school. I didn't even wait until I'd met with Becca and Samara outside, before ripping the first one open. I couldn't seem to get enough. I must've been lacking in some kind of vitamin or mineral. I tossed the empty bag and started in on the next one before making my way outside.

"Are you eating dulse?" Samara said as I approached.

"Yeah, I know. It's weird. I have this super-strong craving."

"My mom had that when she was pregnant with my little brother," Becca said, then paused with this horrified look in her eyes.

I sat down beside her and punched her in the arm. "As if." I'd never had a real boyfriend and they knew it. I pushed more dulse chips in my mouth.

I scanned the area looking for Tor and inadvertently locked eyes with Colby. He took this as an invitation to join our table. He mumbled something to his jocks and strolled over.

Samara and Becca both raised an eyebrow. They often employed their misguided Cupid skills on me and Colby, and it had wrecked our friendship. Or at least, seriously altered it.

In February, after months of Becca and Samara's subliminal signals they'd sent to him causing him to falsely believe I was interested, Colby had given me a Valentine's Day card with chocolates. I *knew* when I opened the box of candy at school that he'd just ruined everything. It took a nanosecond for the rumor mill to start. Colby loved Dori. Aw, it was so cute. Until Dori rejected Colby. Bad Dori.

Around that same time my hair had turned green. After years of chlorine abuse, my light blond hair had become the color of my nana's old copper pot. It took a dose of hair magic by the most expensive hair salon in Saint John to fix that mess.

That was when I started wearing the ugly swim cap. It was also when Colby started calling me *Seaweed* instead of his usual Seward. I chose to believe that it had turned into a term of endearment since. It annoyed me, but if I let him know that, he'd never stop.

SOMEONE TOSSED a Frisbee around and Colby jumped up to

play. To my surprise I spotted Tor in the group. Athletics was another obvious gift the boy had.

And I admitted, watching him play didn't hurt my eyes. At all.

Tor glanced our way, but I couldn't tell if he was looking at me specifically. I didn't want to chance a wave, but I offered a smile just in case.

The guys took a break and ended up at our table. Point for Dori! So sorry Tiffany—I couldn't help but throw a pretend apologetic look her way. Tor didn't sit next to me, though. He sat at one end, closer to Sawyer who was blatantly staring at Tor's arms. His shirt had ridden up from the sweat, and I could see blue marks peeking out on his biceps. Bruises? Was his uncle a beater?

Sawyer saw them too. "Hey dude, are those tats?"

Yeah, maybe they were sexy tattoos, not bruises.

Tor adjusted his shirt. "Kind of."

"Wow," Sawyer said, eyes filling with admiration. "Your parents let you get a tattoo? Let's see it."

Tor stood. "Actually, it's no big deal."

It got silent and tense around the table. He broke it up by adding, "Hey, I have to go, but thanks for the game," then he headed back into the school.

Why'd he just leave like that? Was he embarrassed?

"Do you really think that was a tattoo?" Becca said.

I hated to mention it, but I wanted to know if anyone else thought what I had. "They weren't bruises, were they?"

"Nah," Mike said. "Those were tattoos. My brother has a bunch, but obviously Tor hit a better parlor than my brother did. My brother's look like crap next to his."

Becca said, "Isn't he kind of young for tattoos?"

"I wonder why he wouldn't show them to us," Samara added.

I was wondering the same thing.

"Maybe he's just shy. Or humble," said Becca. "We're just not used to seeing that trait much around here."

Mike threw the Frisbee at her. She caught it and proudly snubbed him—so much for humility.

6

I got up early every morning in order to take Sidney for a walk before school. This was love in action on my part—I wasn't a morning person. I slapped my alarm like a flapping baby bird begging for more time before dragging myself out of bed. The sun was shining brightly and that lifted my mood. I chose my sweat shorts and a hoodie to go for our run, grateful that my legs seemed to have normalized. I pulled my hair back into a ponytail. Ouch. A batch of small lumps had formed behind each ear. Pimples? I rubbed them with my fingers; the whole area was swollen and tender. I'd really have to scrub with shampoo when I showered later.

I energized with a glass of juice then called Sidney to the front door, bending down to give his neck a rub.

"Good morning, Sid." His wet tongue slid up my nose and his bad doggy breath blasted my face. "Ew, Sidney, that's gross."

We had a large half-acre lot with a narrow strip of forest that separated our house from the ocean. Sidney bounded happily down the dirt path with me jogging to keep up.

We had come to the end of the path that opened up to a rocky beach when I heard a strange noise. Sidney stopped and whimpered, pawing at his ears.

I cocked my head and concentrated on the sound. Not quite the song of a dolphin or whale, and certainly not the bird-song or chirping of a forest creature. It had a strange musical clicking pattern that tickled my ears. Its tone and cadence were foreign to me.

Sidney's whimpers grew louder. "Shh, Sidney." I patted his head. He followed me a few steps farther, my sneakers crunching down on the pebbly beach. I paused and peeked around a soft bend.

Through the rising mist I saw Tor in the distance, sitting on a smooth water worn boulder, facing the ocean. He wore blue jeans and no sandals, just bare feet.

His T-shirt lay on the sand.

I held my breath and this time I knew I was doing it. Tor was bare-chested. I could see the contours of all his muscles— pecs, shoulders, abs. He had a swimmer's body, fit and lean, and though beautiful, it wasn't what had made me gasp with wonder.

It was his tattoos. They covered his shoulders, falling half way down his biceps, like inky lace looping down his chest.

First of all, I still couldn't believe his parents or uncle would let an underaged teenager get so many tattoos, and secondly, I couldn't believe how beautiful they were.

I'd seen Mike's older brother's tattoos, and they were nothing like this. John's were a dull, ugly blackish green and red.

Tor's had an effervescent quality. The greens, blues and pinks shimmered in the sun like jewels.

Kind of like...fish scales.

The clicking music continued. Was it coming from Tor? I

tilted my head. The melody was clear, piercing through the rhythmic roar of the waves slapping ashore.

Yup, I was right. The unusual musical clicking was coming from him. Sidney pressed his body down on the pebbles, and barked.

The clicking stopped.

I bent down and spoke sharply into Sidney's ear. "Stop it. Lie down." When I looked up again, Tor had his shirt on, all his beautiful tattoos hidden away. He was looking my direction.

"Hi, Dori." Tor climbed over the rocks and jumped onto the sand beside me. I knew he was wondering what I'd just heard and seen. I was determined not to give that away.

"Oh, hi. Didn't see you there." I tucked my hands in my pockets and rocked on my shoes, feeling awkward, like I'd interrupted something personal. "Sidney and I aren't used to sharing our beach."

"Your beach?"

"Well, not technically, but practically. You know what I mean."

And suddenly I was mortified. My legs had abruptly turned blood red, like that time at swim club and were incredibly itchy. I tried to ignore it.

"We don't usually meet up with people here. Due to the lack of toe grabbing sand. We like that about it."

"I like this strip of beach, too," Tor said. "For the same reasons you do."

Man, not only were my legs flaring and itchy, the lumps behind my ears were burning. I pushed loose strands of hair behind my ears and tried to itch the bumps nonchalantly.

I didn't want to look at my legs because I was afraid it would draw his attention to them. I felt like I was shedding a second skin. What was the matter with me? I leaned against the rocks, hoping to hide them.

"So, you must live close by, then."

Tor nodded and turned to look the direction he'd come from. "Up shore a ways."

While his head was turned I took the opportunity to scratch behind my ears, and then give my legs a go. I felt like a dog with fleas. Why, when I was finally alone with Tor and having a normal conversation did I have to go rabid?

I didn't see him look back at me. I was dying. He'd caught me scratching! Please just dig a hole and bury me now.

His eyes narrowed and I was sure he was going to make up some excuse and bolt. I would if I were him. *More than friends* was probably a big turn off right about now.

"When do you turn sixteen?" he said instead. Like that mattered at this moment. I was working up a sweat with all this itching and nerves. I unzipped my hoodie and took it off, forgetting that I only had a tank top on underneath.

"Um, this summer, the end of next month."

Please look away again so I can scratch. I felt myself squirm, and as much as I wanted to stay with Tor, I just had to get away. Before I could say anything Tor pointed to my shoulder.

"What happened?"

I looked down. A bruise was forming. "Uh, I don't know. I must've run into something." Insane itchiness. "I have to go, Tor. Um, I need to get ready for school."

"Hey, did you want to do something sometime?"

He was asking me on a date? *Now?*

"Yeah, sure. Uh, we could go sailing? My family has a great little boat."

He breathed in deeply and pursed his lips, uncertainty overtaking his face.

Then I remembered the whole jumping-in-the-ocean

fiasco. Maybe that incident had freaked him out more than he let on.

"Or, we could do something else," I said. Anything, as long as I could leave and scratch my skin off first.

"Okay," he said, finally. "The weather's great for sailing."

I breathed out in relief. "Meet me at the pier today at four."

I jogged home as fast as I could, scratching at my legs the whole way.

7

*S*amara and I entered our English class for our final exam. Sawyer leaned against a desk, his hand flapping through the air as he talked, like he had news. "Crazy Jim Macdonald swears he saw one."

"He's usually half drunk," Mike said. "There's a reason why they call him crazy, y' know?"

"I know he's crazy," Sawyer said. "Just never heard him weave a whopper like that before."

"Well, maybe he believes it, but that doesn't mean it's true," Mike said. "It could've been something else."

"What's going on?" I dropped my bag on my desk and sat down.

"Sawyer got accosted by Crazy Jim. Apparently we have a mermaid on the loose in the bay."

I shook my head and threw Sawyer a skeptical look. "You believe something Crazy Jim said? You're as crazy as he is."

"He was pretty convincing." Sawyer's excitement morphed into something more like sheepishness. "Apparently she had long, red hair and a load of jewels around her neck."

I scoffed. "Did she wear a seashell bra?"

"Poor Crazy Jim." Samara clucked her tongue.

"If he did see anything, it was probably a dolphin or sturgeon," I said. "They can look mythical, especially at twilight if the water is rough."

I RUSHED DOWN to the marina after school. Main Street in Eastcove ran parallel to the beach and all the commercial establishments were located on that strip. The general store, the fish market, a scattering of restaurants, the gift shops that popped up on the boardwalk over the summer, and the farmer's market—they all ran along four blocks facing the ocean including the two marinas with their sailboats and fishing vessels painted in bright, primary colors.

My flip-flops made smacking noises on the wooden dock. I stopped when I came to our sailboat, a seventeen foot Vanguard Nomad with a white and blue hull. It didn't scream opulence like some of the larger and newer boats at the pier did, only fitting four or five passengers, tops, but I loved it because it was compact. It was the only boat we'd ever owned and it felt like a member of the family.

The nylon line that ran from our boat to the dock had a lot of slack to account for the tide. There were times when the tide was all the way out and the boats actually rested on the ocean floor. There was enough water now to push out, but I'd use the little motor to get us far enough away from the pier and the other boats, so I didn't accidentally knock into them. Once we were far enough out and into the wind, I'd rely solely on the sails to get us wherever we wanted to go.

I wore surfer shorts and a tank top with a white long sleeve shirt opened over it. My hair was pulled back into a messy updo and I had sunglasses on to cut the glare.

Before I'd left my house I'd slathered on the lotion Mom gave me— my red leg problem, and my behind the ear patches, came and went, but the cream helped—and then topped it off with thirty-block sunscreen.

I did a quick visual check to make sure all the lines and rigging were untangled and that all the shackles and pins securing the lines to the hull were in place.

Just as I was about to pull the ropes out of the cleats and winches, Tor showed up dressed like he was about to head into a mosquito-infested jungle instead of the open sea. He wore blue jeans tucked into rubber boots, a long sleeve shirt buttoned up and wide sunglasses that covered most of his face.

I couldn't help but laugh.

"Hi to you, too," he said.

"I'm sorry," I said, watching him stand stiffly on the dock. "Come aboard."

Tor climbed on and began working proficiently on the jib sail.

"For someone who clearly looks uncomfortable on a boat, you seem to know what you're doing."

Tor shrugged, then untied the rope that had us secured to the dock. I started the motor, pointing the boat out to sea. Once we were clear of the dock and other boats, I cut the engine and hoisted the main sail. Tor hoisted the jib sail. I couldn't help the cheesy thought that crossed my mind: *We made a great team.*

Out on the bay, I felt giddy. The crisp, saline wind on my face, hair flapping, the rolling and rocking of the waves—it was home to me. I was almost just as at ease on the water as I was in it. I had been sailing since before I could walk. I could do this in my sleep.

Tor rested up against the edge looking as handsome as ever, despite the get up. We got out to the middle of the bay, far enough that the people on the shore looked like specks. I turned the rudder until we were crosswind, which slowed us down considerably. Tor lowered the mainsail and then the jib. We were far enough off shore and the tide was at a level where I could safely lower the anchor.

"We're staying awhile?" Tor said.

"I like to take a break when I'm hungry. I brought tuna sandwiches." I opened the cooler. "Do you like tuna? I didn't even think."

"Love it."

I handed him one. Just as he was about to take it, I pulled my hand back.

"First you have to take your shirt off."

I gasped. It sounded like I wanted to play a stripping game. I felt my cheeks burn. "I didn't mean it like that!"

The shock on his face morphed into a smirk. "What did you mean?"

"Just, that you're overdressed for this party. Loosen up a bit."

Tor didn't move. I gripped his sandwich as he held my gaze. It seemed like a really big deal to him.

Then I remembered the tattoos. He probably didn't want me to see them. Maybe if he knew that I knew, he wouldn't care.

"I know about your tattoos."

He raised his eyebrows.

"I mean if that's what you're worried about. I saw them when you had your shirt off at the beach this morning. It's okay. I won't tell anyone."

But, I didn't promise I wouldn't stare. Which was a good thing.

He slowly unbuttoned his shirt and I felt the sandwich in my hand quiver. I put it down on the cooler in front of him.

I stared.

With the reflection off the water, his tattoos were unbeliev-able. They were fluid, little rivers of blue and green running in a lacy Celtic pattern.

"They're beautiful, Tor. Where did you get it done?"

"Hey, I already took my shirt off." He grinned abashedly and I could tell he was embarrassed. "I should at least get to eat before you bombard me with questions."

"Oh, of course. It's on the cooler."

We ate in silence, and I contemplated Tor—how he was dressed today, almost like he was determined not to get wet, how he'd freaked out at the bonfire when I'd tossed the water in his face, the way he'd dove into the sea and never re-surfaced, his beautiful scale-like tattoos...

And then I had the craziest thought.

Nah, that was stupid.

But....

Dori, be real.

Well, he did dive into the ocean and not come out.

So, it was dark; the current dragged him to another beach.

He was "afraid" of water.

Lots of people were afraid of the ocean.

And, I didn't believe in myths.

Still...

It all kind of made sense.

Just because you didn't believe in something, did it auto-matically make it untrue?

I couldn't reel in this fantastical train of thought. My mind knew enough not to name what it was thinking.

But, what about Crazy Jim? Had he spun a tale? Or really seen a tail?

My mouth felt dry, bread gumming up under my lips.

Tor's tattoos danced in the ocean's reflection. He settled his sea green eyes on me, so deep, so otherworldly... and suddenly I believed it.

I choked on my sandwich.

"Are you okay?" Tor said.

I nodded and took a bottle of water from the cooler, turning away from Tor as I slugged it down.

"I'm fine."

I tried to relax with the rocking of the waves. Tor was a merboy. I was sure of it. A freaking merboy. I was thankful for my sunglasses, because they kept Tor from seeing my wide-eyed, freaked out expression, at how much I kept staring at him.

"What are you thinking about?" he said finally.

"Nothing."

"You're very quiet, suddenly. And tense. You're thinking about something."

After a quick inner debate, I decided to test my theory. "Well, actually, I'm thinking about something Sawyer said in English, this morning. Crazy Jim, he's like Eastcove's town drunk. Well, he ran into Sawyer and told him this fantastic story. He believes he saw a mermaid." I watched for Tor's reaction. He didn't flinch but I noticed his mouth twitch slightly.

"That's funny," he said, evenly. "What made you think of that?"

"You."

"Me?"

"Yes, you. You and your unnatural tattoos, you and your aversion to water, you know, while you're dry. You and your late night dive and disappearance into the ocean."

"Lots of people like to believe in myths. Sailors have claimed to see mermaids for centuries. No one has ever proven that they're real."

"You're not denying it, though."

"I got my tattoos done in Boston. I was afraid of badly sanitized needles so I went to the very best, elitist parlor. Same place the stars get theirs done."

"Those must've cost a bundle."

"I got an inheritance rather suddenly."

Oh. Was that what had happened to his parents? I felt very foolish. "I'm sorry."

I turned away and looked out at the horizon. The merfolk theory had made sense for a few minutes. Now I felt like an absolute idiot. A merboy—how ridiculous. I felt so stupid; I was too ashamed to even look at him.

And if that weren't bad enough, my legs started to act up. I scratched my thighs and then the itching started behind my ears.

"Let's go swimming," I said, throwing off my long sleeve shirt. Before Tor had a chance to say anything, I dove in.

The water felt great. Cool, but the summery weather had warmed things up a little. It was definitely warmer than the night Tor dove in.

And it was therapeutic to my flaring red legs and to my embarrassed soul. I swam and dove underwater playfully like a dolphin, happy and at home in the ocean. I surfaced and looked up at Tor who was leaning over the edge with a frown on his face.

"Come on in," I sang, desperate to change the mood. "The water is fine."

He didn't crack a smile. "Come back in the boat, Dori."

"Why? I'm not going to drown. I'm an excellent swimmer. I tried to save you, remember? Come in." I put on my flirty voice. "I'll save you again if you need saving."

"You can save me up here if you want. Just come back in."

I didn't understand him at all. This guy was nothing if not an enigma. Maybe his midnight experience had trauma-tized him. Maybe he really was afraid of water now and that was why he was hesitant to say yes when I invited him sailing.

I decided to give him a break and stroked toward the ladder on the side of the hull.

I felt a pull on my leg.

I was tugged underwater for a moment then bobbed back up. I couldn't think of what my leg was tangled in, but I felt something gripping my foot. We were too far out for seaweed, too far north for most sharks. Plus, I thought a shark bite would hurt a little more than this.

Whatever it was tugged me under again. I opened my eyes, trying to see what was gripping my leg. The water was murky, but it looked like...

A hand.

I kicked my leg now wanting to surface and get a breath. Someone was scuba diving, and the joke wasn't funny!

I heard a splash, or rather felt it, the water around me sloshing. I could hold my breath for a long time, but my chest was burning. If I didn't surface and get a breath soon, I was going to take a big, life-threatening drink.

I saw a streak of blue, large and scaly.

The hand on my leg released and I thrust myself up toward the sunlight.

"Dori!" Tor was in the water with me. His tattoos were shimmering and moving like mad. His eyes were wide and glossy. He was frightened, but I wasn't sure of what. The water? The scuba diver?

I caught my breath and then reached out to him, touching the smooth skin on his back. My hand slipped below the surface. I felt scales.

On Tor. He had a tail.

8

My head felt like cotton candy and I sputtered as the water washed over my face. Tor reached his arm under mine, and he swam back to the boat with me. By the time I gripped the ladder my head had cleared. I hung on, staring hard at Tor. His worried expression hadn't changed.

"I have to go."

I nodded, too stunned to speak.

"Can you get the boat back alone?"

I nodded again. I crawled aboard with shaky legs. He didn't say anything when I caught his eye. Then he disappeared under the water and I knew he wouldn't come back.

I lay on the deck of the boat, letting it rock my nerves back to a manageable tremble. I shivered under my towel until the sun warmed me up.

Tor *was* a merboy. I had been right. I remained in a stupor, my mind unable to process what I'd just seen. It was one thing to imagine that a guy was a merboy, and a whole other thing to witness it as fact.

Tor had rescued me from the stupid scuba guy and by

doing so he was forced to reveal his true nature. Not just to me but possibly to the scuba guy. If that moron saw him through the murkiness, it would be big news in Eastcove by the time I got back.

What now? Would Tor and his uncle have to leave? Was that why they'd left Maine?

Thinking about Tor leaving Eastcove produced a dull ache in my chest. I didn't want him to leave. Despite what I knew, despite what he *was*, I still really liked him and I cared about what might happen to him.

Was there a way I could help Tor and his uncle? Defuse the story? Convince everyone once again, that it was a trick of the light?

And would Tor *want* me to help them? Did he still want *me*?

Finally dried and over the initial shock, I pulled up the anchor. I reset the sails and headed back to Eastcove. When I'd left the shore earlier, I was with Tor. Now I was returning back to the pier alone.

I stumbled along Main Street in a daze. I somehow made it home and spent the rest of the evening in my room, faking a cough, using illness as an excuse to be left alone. Crosby purred in my ear as I tried to figure things out. Tried to figure Tor out.

How did animorphism work? Or actually, partial animorphism which–if you believe in that kind of thing–and I did now, had to hurt. Or at least be really uncomfortable.

Obviously, when Tor had two legs he didn't like water, so I was guessing water was a trigger. If Tor got wet, he morphed.

I wasn't sure how it worked for him to get his legs back, but since he didn't get out of the water with me, it must have been a more difficult process.

What I hadn't yet considered were the questions Tor was likely posing to himself. Maybe Tor only wanted something with me as long as I didn't know his secret. He *did* make up that story about Boston. Those tattoos definitely didn't come from a tattoo parlor, no matter how elite.

I wondered if he'd show up for school tomorrow, if I'd ever see him again.

Just before dusk, I called Sidney and headed out to the beach. I searched for Tor, going back to the rock I'd dubbed Tor's Rock, and felt a brooding emptiness when he wasn't there. I traveled a good distance in each direction, finally giving up when it got too dark.

I lay awake on my bed, my heart growing heavier with each hour. Now that I worried that Tor might be gone from my life for good, I longed to see him again. Maybe seeing him with a tail was a deal killer. I slept fitfully and when dawn broke, I slipped out of the house, careful not to wake Mom or Dad, hoping that he would be looking for me, too.

With Sidney on my heels I was soon at the water's edge. The fog was dense and low and I couldn't see the horizon. I headed north toward the bend that hid Tor's Rock from view. My heart thumped with anticipation. Please, let him be there.

I rounded the bend. The mist settled in eerie patches and I could barely make out the rock. Then I saw movement. I hadn't realized I'd been holding my breath. I let it out in a slow, shudder. I froze to the spot. Tor was there. With legs on.

He spotted me. His eyes widened with question. I felt that sense of embarrassment that manifests when you've accidentally caught someone who forgot to lock the bathroom door, and meet up with them the next day. I felt myself flush.

It seemed neither of us knew what to do. Even Sidney was confused. He squirmed a bit then nestled into the pebbles to wait it out.

Tor took a step and my legs suddenly came to life. We moved toward each other and it felt like a hazy dream.

"I was hoping that you'd come." Tor's voice was smooth and yet there was a question, a trace of insecurity there.

"I came yesterday."

The corner of his mouth tugged up in a smile. He shoved his hands into his pockets. "Well, this is awkward."

I mimicked him by storing my hands away, too. "Yup."

He motioned with his head. "Want to walk?"

"Okay."

The tide was out so we were in no danger of accidentally getting our feet wet, but I stayed on the inside just to make sure. Sidney lagged behind. We scared up a flock of seagulls and they squawked and circled us in noisy protest.

"I imagine you have a few questions," Tor said softly.

"A few."

"Shoot."

I didn't know where to start. "Um, how long have you been... like this?"

"I am merfolk. I've been coming ashore for almost a year."

He was *merfolk*. Merfolk were real. I shook my head.

"Dori?"

"How often are you... like this?" Boy, my questions were lame.

"You mean human-like?"

I nodded.

"About half and half. I have to go into the sea every few days or so, otherwise I dehydrate."

Okay. I gave myself a minute to process that. "What did you mean when you said you've only been coming to shore for almost a year?"

Tor paused. "It's a choice we have at a certain age. I made the choice to come to shore."

"You mean to get legs?"

"Yeah."

I still didn't fully understand, but I decided to question him more on that later. Right now I was wondering why he was here in Eastcove with his uncle.

"What really happened to your parents?"

"They're still alive. It's just that they live underwater."

"They're not like you?"

"No. If you don't choose to come ashore when you're an adolescent, and not many do, the ability passes."

"Why did you choose it then? Don't you miss your parents?"

He shrugged. "I guess you could call it wanderlust. And yes, I do miss them, but we communicate."

The musical clicking? Kind of like aquatic email?

"Do you have brothers and sisters?"

"An older brother. His name is Kon."

"Does Kon come to shore sometimes?"

"No. He chose not to."

I thought about his family and how I'd never meet them or ever be invited to dinner. I wondered if Tor would bother telling them about me.

"I know you work hard at keeping your existence secret. What if that scuba diver tells everyone he saw you that way?"

He squinted at me. "What scuba diver?"

"The guy who grabbed my foot and pulled me under. The reason you had to dive in to rescue me."

A dark shadow passed over Tor's face.

"That is why you jumped in, isn't it? To rescue me?"

"Yes."

"Well, thank you for that."

"Please, don't mention it."

"So, what about that guy?"

Tor looked off into the distance. "My kind has a way of

blending in with our watery surroundings and disappearing from sight. Which is why we're never caught."

"But you're seen sometimes, otherwise we wouldn't know about you at all."

"That's true."

"And what about the redheaded mermaid that Crazy Jim Shaw?" I felt bad now for mocking him. "Why didn't she blend in?"

"Ah, Shava. She's kind of immature. A little too naive you could say."

"Shava?"

"She's my cousin."

Tor stopped suddenly, boring his bright eyes into mine. "Dori, you can't tell anyone. Ever." He leaned in closer. I felt his breath on my cheek. "Please, promise me."

I didn't hesitate. "I'll never tell."

He didn't pull back. I thought he might kiss me. My first kiss here on the beach with a merboy! My heart skipped like a stone across water and I swallowed hard. His hand lightly brushed my cheek. I trembled.

He leaned in, but our lips didn't meet. Instead he rested his forehead on mine and took my hand, weaving his fingers through mine. This wasn't like how he held my hand the first time we met. This was intimate. I felt like I was having an out-of-body experience. A very pleasant one.

"What are we going to do now, Dori?" he whispered.

I couldn't speak because my heart was lodged solidly in my throat. It was a good question. What *were* we going to do now?

9

Samara, Becca and I huddled together under an overhang by the front entrance at school the next morning. Though it was raining, it was warm and we didn't want to spend any more time inside than we had to.

"Only two days left!" Becca said. "It feels like an eternity."

"I know." Samara fiddled with her bracelets. "The last days of school always drag by."

I reached out past the overhang and let the drizzle fall on my hand. Was it wet enough out to keep Tor away? My chest tightened at the thought of not seeing him.

"Hello, Earth to Dori." Samara snapped her fingers.

"Oh, sorry."

"What's with you today?" she continued. "You seem kind of spaced out."

I tried not to glance over her shoulder too much. "No I'm good. Really. How was your guys' weekend?"

Becca went off on how busy it got this time of year on her farm, and that she barely had time to sneak away to go to the library, but I couldn't focus. Tor had just come into view and I felt the pull of a smile on my lips. He was dressed head to toe in rubber—boots, rain jacket with his hood pulled over his head covering his face, and oversized gloves on his hands.

Becca and Samara turned to see what I was staring at.

"He may be good looking," Samara said, shaking her head, "but man, that boy is strange."

"No kidding," Becca said. "Doesn't he know how dorky he looks?"

Tor stopped when he reached us in the dry zone. He peeled off his gloves and pushed his hood back—his smoldering looks overwhelming me. He greeted Samara and Becca with a polite hello and then stared hard and meaningfully at me. "Hey."

I nibbled my bottom lip, suddenly shy. "Hey."

"See you in Earth science, Dori."

"See you." He walked away and I was wrecked. Totally smitten.

"What was *that*?" Samara spat out.

"Yeah," said Becca. "That was kind of steamy. Hey, did you guys hook up or something?"

"No, well, not like that. We met up at the beach yesterday."

"But you didn't hook up?" Samara said, her eyebrow raised high.

"Not yet. He's the kind of guy that likes to take things slow."

"But he likes you?"

"Yes."

"And you like him?"

"Absolutely."

"Wow, Dori," Becca said dreamily. "You did it."

Yes, I did. A big sappy smile overtook my face.

"Did I miss something here?" Samara said, beads clicking together when she spun around. "You need to spill, girl."

Thankfully, the bell rang. There were too many secrets I couldn't tell them.

Finally, the day ended. I'd found it hard to concentrate in all of my classes and virtually impossible in Earth science, knowing Tor was behind me staring at my head. Tiffany obviously still thought she had a chance with Tor because her flirting skills were on full display. I'd caught Tor's eye and he winked at me, sending little sparkly shivers down my spine.

I was at my locker when Tor met up with me.

"Hey, there." He leaned against the locker beside mine and I choked with giddiness that he was there waiting as I grabbed my things.

"Are you busy now?" he asked.

"Not really. Swim club is tomorrow, so I'm free." School might've been ending but swim club at this level went year round.

"Can you come over?"

"To your place?" It was weird but I still didn't know exactly where Tor lived, and suddenly I desperately wanted to go there. "Yes, I can."

He smiled and I loved how easy it was to make him happy. I closed my locker door and we fell into stride beside each other.

I almost had a heart attack when he reached for my hand.

This was it. Public declaration!

More than a few heads turned when they saw us, and I got the feeling that this must be what it was like to walk the red carpet. I passed Samara and Becca, who, after reining in their shocked looks, gave me a stealthy thumbs up.

Tiffany didn't regain control of her stunned expression.

Dori Seward had never been any real kind of competition for her before now.

Colby's face flashed with surprise and then anger. Like they said, if looks could kill, Tor would be broiled steak.

I did feel kind of bad about Colby, but it just wasn't meant to be. I'd have to forget about him. Tor and I were together now.

The rainy system had blown over and bright sunshine filtered through the patchy gray skies. I was relieved. Walking around hand in hand with Tor in his rubber suit wouldn't have been nearly as victorious.

We headed to the beach and then north. I held my sandals in my hand, enjoying the grind of the sand between my toes. Tor did the same.

"I thought I knew every inch of this beach," I said, trying to picture a cabin on the shore. "I'm surprised I haven't seen your uncle's place before."

"It's pretty well hidden."

He wasn't kidding. He led me farther up the beach, over craggy rocks, and animal trails through the forest pressing into the tide line. We came to a steep crevice that filled to overflowing at high tide. The Bay of Fundy had the highest tides in the world. It was like a gigantic washtub that emptied and filled every day; the tide could get as high as two stacked houses.

You needed the sure-footedness of a mountain goat to get down. Tor took my bag and gripped my hand, helping me to descend in one piece.

"I can see now, why no one knows where you live."

"We do it on purpose, as you can understand."

Finally, we entered a narrow opening in the cliff. We climbed some more until it opened up into a cavernous space.

"You live in a cave?"

Tor smiled slyly. "It works for us."

The passage was lit by oil lamps. Nothing exotic, just the

ordinary Coleman camping types. Soon we came to a room that made me hum. It was a cave style RV. All the camping furnishings were there: foldable table and chairs, camp stove with propane, a portable sink with dishes drying in a rack. Two foldable cots, neatly made. Daylight streamed in from a hole in the ceiling, and the whole effect was very homey.

"Cool," I said. "This is every kid's dream."

"I like it."

"What do you do when it rains?" I motioned to the skylights.

"We cover them up with tarps."

Of course. In the corner, under a smaller skylight, was a desk with a laptop opened on it.

"You get internet?"

"Yeah. But you have to be set up right under that hole. It picks up wireless."

"Amazing." I walked over to look at the maps taped to the wall. Instead of land maps like most people had, these were maps of the oceans of the world.

"We study the oceans like your people study land geography."

I frowned at the term "your people". It separated us, somehow.

"I've often thought of becoming an oceanographer," I said. "I love the ocean and I love to swim so it seems like a good fit."

"I'm sure you'd be excellent at it."

"You could probably teach me a lot."

I heard the scuffing of footsteps. A familiar voice called out, "Tor?"

"Uncle Dex," Tor answered. "We have company."

Dex hadn't lost his dominating demeanor. I didn't know who was more surprised. Dex, that Tor had brought a friend home, or me that Tor hadn't told his uncle that he planned to bring me home. Thankfully, his hardy face broke into a smile.

"Hello," Dex said, reaching out his hand. "We've met before, haven't we?"

"Yes." I shook his hand. It was massive. "At the police station."

"Ah, that's right. Well, that was an unfortunate turn of events, but thankfully everything worked out fine. You'll stay for dinner?"

I hadn't expected an invitation, and it took me a moment to respond. "Yeah, I'd love to, but I'd have to let my mom know. Will my cell phone work here?"

Tor nodded. "You have to go outside to get reception."

He led me through a rudimentary staircase carved out of the dirt that took us outside. I stood in the open air in awe. The horizon reached out into infinity, the surface of the ocean alive with movement. The remnant rays of the sun setting in the west bounced off the water like a shimmering blanket. It was breathtaking.

And private. The rocks in front of the cave kept the boats and the swimmers away. It was very secluded. A perfect secret spot.

"Did you and your uncle create this yourselves?"

Tor shook his head. "Some of our kind from the sea who can morph the way we do found it years ago. Uncle Dex and I fixed it up to suit us. We're the only ones living here right now."

"Wanderlust?"

"That and the fact that we need someone to track what's going on in the world above the sea. You can imagine, but the choices humans make have a big impact on our world."

I was curious. "Like?"

"Over fishing, deep sea drilling, oil spills, pollution. You saw the garbage patch video. The more we know about human activity the more we can counteract."

I was embarrassed to be human when he rattled off that list. "And how do you counteract?"

Tor's face grew somber. "To be honest, there's not much we can do, except adapt. Move."

"Does your uncle know that I know?"

"Yes, I had to tell him. We keep track of everyone who discovers our secret. It's important to our survival."

An uncomfortable thought nagged me. I wondered what the root of Tor's interest was in me. Did he really actually like me? Or was he just keeping track of me?

I called my mother. She was a little surprised, especially since she'd never met Tor, only knew him by reputation and of course, his nighttime swimming escapade. I told her I'd bring him over soon so she and Dad could meet him, and that I'd be home before dark.

"So, what's for supper?" I asked with a smile. "What do merguys eat for dinner?"

I was sure it would be beneficial that I liked seafood and dulse.

"Ah, you'll be pleasantly surprised."

We spent a moment gazing at the view, watching the fishing vessels patrol. A pod of dolphins jumped playfully in the distance.

"When you dive into the ocean, you become a merboy," I began.

"Merman."

Merman, not merboy. Duly noted. "Uh, sorry, you become a merman. How does it work the other way? How do you become a human man?"

"My body is more comfortable in its merman form, so transitioning that way is easier, happens in mere seconds. It's more of a process the other way. I have to pull myself out of the water onto one of the rocks over there."

He pointed and I saw an outcropping of smooth water-worn rocks that dotted the shoreline. "It's easier if it's high tide, and it's better if it's dark. Even though this area is well protected, we can still be spotted by satellite."

Satellite? I'd never thought about that.

"Then I have to wait until I dry out. Once I'm dry, it just happens. My legs form."

"Does it hurt?"

"Yeah," he said, reluctantly. "It's not something I'd want you to see. But, it's worth it to me. No one forces me to do this."

Then I asked the burning question. "Do you think you'll ever stop?"

"I don't know."

I couldn't keep the concern off my face. Tor stroked my cheek, sending little fireworks down my back. I wanted him to kiss me. Really, really wanted him to kiss me.

He gazed at me oddly, a glint in his eye, dimples forming around a grin. He leaned in slowly. I stopped breathing. This was it—my first kiss. He gently rubbed his lips against mine, and little tingles swam down my arms and chest and throughout my body.

His lips were soft and full with a delicious hint of saltiness. If this was how Tor wanted to keep track of me, I didn't mind.

"Enough serious talk," he said quietly, pulling away. "Let's go eat before Uncle Dex sics the sharks on us."

I nodded, numbly. Food was the furthest thing from my mind.

School ended with more of a whimper than a bang. The next day I'd started picking strawberries at Becca's farm. It was exhausting work, but I got to meet up with Tor at the beach afterward on the days I didn't go into Saint John for swim club. Usually we grabbed a fruit smoothie and sat on the dock—me with my feet dangling in the water, Tor with his legs crossed safely on deck. Just sitting next to him was energizing.

When the strawberries were finished, I spent most of my working hours helping Becca at her fruit stand on the boardwalk, which absolutely came alive during the summer. A myriad of kiosks sprung up from the barren winter beach—souvenir stands with miniature sailboats, dried out sea stars, sunglasses and beach knickknacks; snack shacks with popcorn, hot dogs, soda pop and every kind of beach treat, along with a wide selection of seafood.

The town strung lights along the boardwalk in the summers so that business could continue after dark. Live music, usually

Celtic or folk bands, played regularly on the makeshift stage that was built near the pier every summer.

Tor manned one of the seafood kiosks. I'd wondered how he and his uncle made their money and smiled at the thought of them harvesting mussels, crab and lobster in their private cove. Probably with a very personal touch.

Having Tor at the boardwalk made me happy since I could see him at least once in a while throughout the day. Even though we were spending a lot of after-hours time together, I never got tired of him.

July 1^{ST,} Canada Day, traditionally meant a big sand sculpture contest on the beach. I was good at athletics and pretty strong in academics, but I couldn't draw or do anything artsy to save my life. Because of this I'd never entered, but I always watched and cheered on my more creative friends.

The beach was marked out into sections. Each section had a little red flag staked into the ground with a number. This was where the artist created his or her masterpiece, which was judged by prominent locals including the mayor and the police chief.

Becca and Samara always entered and one year they came in third, which had made them deliriously happy.

The good weather and the national holiday had the tourists out in full force—mostly from Maine and New England, the Eastern Provinces of Canada and a sprinkling from Europe and Asia. I loved this part of summer, when people were dressed in every variety of tacky, and spoke with interesting accents or in languages I didn't understand at all.

I saw Colby take position along with Tiffany as his partner. They'd been hanging out a lot since Tor and I had gotten together. I wasn't sure if they actually liked each other, or if they were just offering each other moral support. Colby's normal reaction to me these days was a squint and a snarl. And even though I tried to keep things friendly, let's just say our backseat rides to Saint John were less than comfortable.

Tor signed up to compete.

"I shouldn't be surprised," I said. "Is there anything you aren't good at?"

"Mountain hiking. I need to stay at sea level."

"Good to know." Not like there were a lot of mountains around Eastcove.

We went to Tor's assigned section, red flag number 31. "Don't mind if I watch, do you?" I said, laying a towel down on the sand.

He smiled knowingly. "Actually, it would help me a lot if you do."

Like a muse? I was happy to be Tor's muse and I meant to enjoy my close up view of Tor while he was at it. I wished he'd take off his shirt so I could admire his six-pack and his tattoos but I knew he wouldn't do that. I felt like merfolk VIP— honored to have had the pleasure of seeing Tor up close.

I shimmied my butt in the sand, getting comfortable. I wore denim shorts and a sea green ribbed tank top. My hair was pulled back in a high ponytail and I had large tortoise shelled rimmed sunglasses on my face. A seashell bracelet dangled from my wrist.

I dug in my beach bag for my sunscreen. Ever since my legs had started erupting I'd been keen to keep the sun's rays from adding damage. A trip to the doctor's office didn't really shed any light on the problem. Dr. Brown had said it wasn't textbook eczema but gave me a prescription for it anyway.

I waved to Samara and Becca who were close by, red flag number 37. "Good luck," I shouted.

I leaned back and turned my face to the sun. The breeze

was cool enough to keep everyone comfortable. I licked the salty mist from the sea off my lips.

Each contestant was provided with a large pail of water to moisten the sand. I was Tor's designated water supplier if he got low.

The mayor blew the whistle and sand flew. The contestants had thirty minutes to create their masterpieces.

I was dying to see what Tor had in mind.

Tor dug like mad, shaping the sand into a long slug-like mold. I wondered if I'd overestimated his artistic abilities. I glanced around at the competition. Becca and Samara were forming what looked like a turtle. I saw several castles sprout up and Colby and Tiffany were building something tall.

Tor piled sand on top of one end of the slug, so it looked like an "L" on its side, with the short side sticking up.

"What are you making?" I asked.

He didn't stop to look at me. "You'll see."

He shaped the top bit now and I could tell it was a head. He worked masterfully, a nose and mouth and sunglasses over the eyes. He ran his fingers through the sand until it became a long mass of wavy hair down the back.

I sat up straight, squinting. I took off my glasses and compared them. Tor shaped the torso, modestly creating a ribbed tank top over the bosom and I felt myself blush. When he fashioned a seashell bracelet over one arm I was certain.

He was sculpting me!

"You'll never win with that," I said.

"I don't care about winning."

Oh, man. I was crazy about this guy! I did my best model at the beach pose with my legs, hoping to help him out a bit.

But he did something different with the legs.

In fact they weren't legs at all.

"You're making me a mermaid?" I swallowed. I didn't know

if I should be flattered or offended. Was this what Tor really wanted? Something I could never give him?

Tor stopped and studied me. "Should I not? I can change it."

I was being silly. "No, that's okay. I like it."

Tor went back to work. I was in awe at his detail. I took a good look at the tail; the scales and muscle pattern were perfect in their detail.

He went back to working on the face and I was amazed at how much it actually looked like me. Only more beautiful.

"I think you're very beautiful," Tor said.

What? How did he do that?

"You are beautiful to me, Dori. With or without a tail."

All I wanted to do now was a lot of PDA, but I restrained myself from throwing myself at him.

The whistle blew and everyone stopped. The winner would be announced later on, just before the fireworks.

"Wow." I couldn't stop saying it. I might not be a sand sculpture judge, and I wasn't saying this because it was supposed to look like me, but Tor's artwork was amazing.

"I'm glad you like it," Tor said. He leaned in and kissed me gently on the cheek. I *melted.*

"We're still on for dinner?" he asked. My parents had insisted that I bring Tor over for the family barbecue later.

"Yeah. Hopefully, they won't be too hard on you."

"I think I can handle whatever they dish out." He brushed his hand clean of sand. "I have to close up the kiosk. Meet me later?"

"Yes, we should definitely show up at my house together." My gaze lingered on him as he left. When he was out of sight, I went to Samara and Becca's section and admired their turtle. It looked just like the surfer dude turtle from *Finding Nemo.*

"That's great you guys," I gushed. "You're both so talented."

"My mother would rather I be talented in algebra like you, Dori," Becca said with a big grin, "but, thanks."

"What did Tor sculpt?" Samara shielded her eyes from the sun and peered down the beach.

"Come see."

I wasn't sure what to make of their expressions and their initial silence made me nervous and embarrassed.

"It's official," Samara said. "He's gone for you."

I couldn't help but giggle when she said that.

"He's a pretty good artist, too," Becca said with admiration. "He's obviously sculpted sand before."

"Well," I said. "He does spend a good amount of time on the beach."

Dad had the barbecue fired up by the time Tor and I slipped into the back yard.

"Hi, sweetie," Mom said. She had a tray in her hand filled with glasses and a pitcher of iced tea.

Tor stepped up to assist. "Let me help you with that."

"Oh, all right." She handed the tray to Tor and looked at me pointedly. "So, are you going to introduce us?"

"Mom and Dad, this is Tor, Tor, my mom and dad."

Tor set the tray down on the patio table. Dad shook Tor's hand with a soft pleased-to-meet-you, then turned back to the barbecue without further inquiry. Dad lacked his usual easy-going smile and I got the distinct impression that he wasn't so crazy about me bringing boyfriend-type guys home.

Mom was far more expressive. "So, glad to finally meet you, Tor. Of course we've heard a lot about you. We're so happy that your incident in the ocean turned out fine."

Mom!

"Thank you, Mrs. Seward. The moss on the rocks makes them very slippery. Climbing them was a dumb thing to do."

Dad piped up. "Not at ease on the ocean, eh?"

Tor shot me a quick sideways glance and I tried not to laugh.

"I guess I could learn a few things."

Mom turned to me. "Nana's in the kitchen, Dori. Go in and help her with the salad, okay?"

I didn't like leaving Tor with my parents, but figured he could take care of himself. The salmon steaks were starting to smell good, and I realized I was hungry.

"Where are Luke and Mark?" I asked on my way up the back steps.

"They should be here any minute," Mom said, dropping cobs of corn into a large pot of boiling water.

Nana was staring out the opened window, obviously spying on all that had just transpired in the back yard.

"Hi, Nana."

"Hi, darling." She reached over and pulled me into a one-arm hug, kissing me on the head before letting me go. "How's my girl?"

"I'm good." I grabbed the carrot peeler and a carrot.

"So, that's your new boy?"

Not like I had an old boy.

"I guess so," I said. Nana wouldn't stop staring out the window. Her brow furrowed as she watched Tor sitting in a lawn chair petting Sidney who seemed to have finally accepted him as a friend. I didn't think she liked the idea of me bringing a boyfriend type boy home either.

"Where did you meet him?"

"At the beach, why?"

Her frown lingered. "No reason." She threw in the

cucumber pieces she'd finished chopping and settled her blue eyes on me.

"Dori, I want you to know that you can talk to me about anything— and I mean anything."

Huh? Oh, no. She wasn't going to give me a sex talk was she?

"Okay," I said nervously. I quickly grabbed the salad bowl. "I'll meet you outside." I wondered if loneliness was getting to Nana. Grandpa *had* been gone for over ten years.

Everyone engaged in *Please pass this, please pass that*, until we all had what we wanted on our plates. This was followed by the muffled sounds of munching with appreciative moans thrown in for good measure. Once the initial hunger was staved off, the conversation began.

"We have Tor and Jolene here," Nana said. "So, where's your girlfriend, Mark?"

"Yeah, where's your girlfriend, Mark," Luke mimicked.

"No time for girls, Nana," Mark said, picking corn from his teeth. "Besides I'm leaving soon. I'll find a girl in Calgary."

"Careful, Mark," Luke jibed. "You're going to make Mom cry."

"I'm already crying," Mom said good-naturedly. "Every night in my pillow. When I'm not stroking his baby picture."

"I'll have to peel your mom off you at the airport," Dad added with a grin. "It's gonna be embarrassing."

"Don't worry, Mom," Luke said. "Tor's here now. Soon you'll forget all about Mark."

I gave Luke the evil eye. That was hardly funny and by the muted laughter, I could tell everyone agreed with me.

"Just joking," Luke said defensively. "By the way, Tor, what was with the big search and rescue thing the other week? Your way of making sure we all get to know the new guy?"

If Luke were closer I would've kick him in the shins. As it was, he still shouted out, "Ow."

"Shut up, Luke," Jolene said. Ah, so she did the kicking. I'd have to thank her later. "You're being an idiot."

"Hey, no offense, man. Just asking. It's not like I'm the only one."

"I slipped off the wet rocks," Tor said politely. "It was an accident."

"Sure man," Luke said. "No big deal. You're all right, that's the main thing."

I jumped in. "Can someone pass the salt?"

We made it through the rest of dinner and all the additional awkward moments. I excused myself and went upstairs. When I returned, I was ready.

"We're going back to the beach," I said, collecting dirty dishes. "I'll be home after the fireworks."

Tor and I walked along the beach where the bonfire had been, hand in hand. I held my sandals in my free hand, enjoying the feeling of sand dragging between my toes.

"Sorry for the inquisition back there," I said.

Tor chuckled. "Actually, I expected worse."

"Luke was in his best worst form, and I don't know what was wrong with Nana."

"They're just protective of you. You're the only girl and the youngest child; I'd be worried if they didn't show concern when you bring boys home."

"I don't bring *boys* home. You're the only boy."

"What about Colby Johnston."

Oh, what did he know about that? Or worse, what did he think he knew?

"He's just a friend, almost like a brother."

"I don't think he sees you as a sister."

"Why do you say that?"

"Guys can tell when they like the same girl. I'm sure it's the same with girls who like the same guy."

He had a point.

"I know Colby likes me," I admitted. "He's told me so, himself. I just don't feel that way about him."

We slowed to a stop and I looked at Tor, working up the courage to present the question I was dying to ask him.

"Well, I'm wondering if it's okay for me to ask you for an early birthday present. I know it's still over three weeks away, but I can't wait."

"Um, okay. What is it?"

"Will you take me swimming?"

"What?"

I knew he heard me; he just couldn't believe what I'd asked for, because we both knew what that meant.

I stared into his bright eyes. "I want to go swimming with you."

"Now?"

"It's starting to get dark and we can go to your cove where it's secluded."

"I see you've thought this through."

"I have. I've got my swimming suit on underneath my clothes."

Tor laughed. "Well, it's not like you haven't seen everything already. Let's go."

He led me expertly through moon-lit darkness. I trusted him with my every step. We got to the steep crevice that concealed his cove and he helped me down. Instead of making our way up to his cave, like before, we stayed on the rocks.

"Are you sure about this?" he asked.

"I'm more than sure." I let my sundress fall to my ankles. I was wearing my red one piece. Tor whistled.

"Oh, stop that."

He laughed and dove in. I watched as he submerged, but he went too deep and many minutes passed before he surfaced.

"What are you waiting for?"

Tingles of excitement shot up my spine and down both my legs. I was about to swim with Tor the merman!

I jumped in and gasped from the cold, but with the way adrenaline was pumping through my veins I soon warmed up. There was enough moonlight reflecting off the water that I could easily make out Tor's face. His eyes were glinting with amusement.

"Let's see what you got."

His tattoos danced in a hypnotizing swirl; I couldn't take my eyes off of them. Then he splashed me with his tail. With his tail! I swam my hardest and could barely keep up. I felt like I was just learning to swim, a complete novice.

Tor laughed and swam my way. He stopped where I treaded water, turning his back to me. "Climb on."

I held on tight and laughed out loud with the thrill of having Tor's body under mine, my arms wrapped securely around his neck. He dipped under water. Tor knew I could hold my breath for several minutes, but I couldn't actually breathe under water. He stayed close to the surface.

"Show off!" I shouted.

He slowed things down then, almost to a stop and pulled me around so we were holding on to each other face to face. I could feel his scales with my toes, the muscular strength of his tail as I wrapped my legs around his body.

He tilted his head and I leaned in, touching his lips with mine. Ocean water mingled with our kisses.

"Is it possible for a merperson to fall in love with a human?" I whispered in between breaths.

"Yes."

"It's happened before?" I was surprised. I really thought those kind of stories were lore.

"It has."

"Good."

We kissed and kissed and kissed, like the world would end if we stopped, until the fireworks shot off. Tor and I scanned the sky and it felt like the fireworks were bursting with color just for us. Then he kissed me again.

"You know," Tor said, his eyes twinkling. "Independence Day fireworks go off in three days, just across the border."

"We may have to come back," I said coyly.

"We may."

11

When we got back to the rocks, Tor hoisted me up but stayed behind in the water.

"Wait for me in the cave."

Though curious about the process of how his tail would shape shift back to legs, I respected his privacy.

Dex had the Coleman lanterns lit so it was easy to find my way in the darkness. I slipped my dress back on before calling out, "Hello?"

Dex appeared in the entrance, his shadow looming like a giant, and I felt momentarily frightened. He probably didn't take trespassing lightly, so I added quickly, "It's Dori. Tor sent me. He's, uh, coming and asked me to wait for him here."

"I see," Dex's low voice rumbled. "Come in, then. Would you like some tea?"

My core body temperature was below comfortable levels and I nodded. Hot tea would be wonderful. Seeing me shiver, Dex handed me a blanket. I wrapped it tightly around my body before sitting in one of the chairs around the table.

"My nephew must think more highly of you than I first imagined."

Yay. Hearing Dex say that made me bubble up inside. "Why do you say that?"

"He's never gone swimming with a human before."

He'd known we were swimming together. I supposed my wet hair and the damp spots on my dress were a giveaway.

"I like him a lot, too."

Dex paused to consider me. "Liking the boy may not be enough."

A dark shot of fear seared me. Was Dex going to ask me to leave Tor alone?

"Maybe it's more than 'like' for me."

Dex poured the boiling water into the teapot, and carried it over along with three matching cups, cream and sugar.

"My dear, I'm afraid you don't know what you're signing up for."

"Why don't you enlighten me?"

He poured for both of us.

"Our life is very complicated."

His explanation was cut short by the sound of someone crying out in pain. My heart dropped. "Tor?"

Dex nodded. "Pain is a prerequisite to the pleasure of being human."

Tor cried out again and I jumped to my feet.

"Dori!" Dex shook his head in warning. "It's almost over. Now, come sit."

I returned to the table, my legs quivering. Tor had known he'd have to endure this tonight when I'd made my request. I felt sick.

I sipped my tea, but I couldn't stop my eyes from darting to the doorway waiting for Tor.

"Like I said," Dex continued, "our lives are very complicated. Tor and I are trying to fit into two opposing worlds. You only understand one."

"I want to understand both," I said quickly.

"I'm sure you do. However, for you it is impossible. Dori, dear, I know I'm asking a lot here, and it's only because I love my nephew…"

My heart plunged to my feet. I didn't want to hear what he was going to say next.

"If you truly care for him like you say, you should let him go."

"Let me go where?" Tor walked in with a bounce to his step. You'd never guess he'd just gone through agony to get those legs.

Dex flashed me a look. He didn't want Tor to know what he'd asked of me.

"Uh, I was just telling Dex about my swim meet coming up this weekend," I said. "It's the Maritimes competition, the lead up to the Junior Nationals. Do you want to come?"

I hadn't planned on inviting Tor. I couldn't imagine what he thought about our human swimming competitions. After swimming with him tonight, he must think they were a joke. "You don't have to," I added. "It's no big deal, really."

"I'd love to," he said with a smile.

Dex handed him his cup of tea, his frown barely concealed.

"My only problem is the humidity in the pool room. I might have, uh, a reaction." Tor blushed and an overwhelming wave of affection for him washed over me. Suddenly, I wanted him there. I wanted him to share my life as much as possible, especially since I couldn't fully share his.

"There's an observation room," I said. "It's behind glass, and very dry."

"Great!" Tor grinned widely.

Dex's mouth pulled down into a deeper frown. I'd just done the exact opposite of what he'd asked of me.

I squirmed under Dex's disapproving gaze. "Uh, I should go, Tor. I told Mom I'd be home after the fireworks."

12

I sat in the middle of the backseat of our family SUV, an older model Ford Escort. Tor was on one side, behind my Dad who drove, and Nana was on the other side behind my mom. Nana smelled heavily of a floral perfume, like she'd just stepped out of her own garden patch.

Mom cranked her head back at us. "How's your uncle?" she said, not waiting for an answer. "It's so strange that we haven't run into him yet. You should bring him around some day."

"He's fine," Tor said. "And I'm sure he'd love to meet you."

"Are your parents coming to Eastcove this summer?" Her eyes moved back and forth between us as though checking to make sure we weren't holding hands or cuddling. We weren't.

"No. I'll be going to Maine soon to see them."

Maine? Like on the coast of Maine? Or like a thousand leagues under the sea off the coast of Maine? And what did he mean by *soon?*

"Oh, that will be nice for you." Mom stared at the road then back at us. "Do you have any brothers or sisters, Tor?"

"An older brother," Tor said. "He's left home."

Mom's eyes blinked quickly like she was trying to think of something else to ask him.

"Oh, give the boy a break, Ann," Nana said, surprising us all. "You're chewing his ear off."

"No I'm not."

Mom turned her attention back to Tor. "It's so nice of you to come along to watch Dori swim." She flashed Nana a warning look.

"I wouldn't miss it," Tor said. "I know that Dori's an excellent swimmer."

"Tor's not too bad himself," I said, grinning.

"Really?" Mom said. "Maybe you should join the swim team?"

"Mom, he already has things he likes to do." I was siding with Nana now. I threw Mom a look that said enough with the hundred questions. She didn't get the hint.

"Like what?"

"Just stuff. Jeez, Mom."

"What's the matter with you two? I'm just trying to get to know your friend better." She turned her eyes back to the road, settling back in her seat with a thump.

Ugg.

"Hey, Dad?" Her behavior embarrassed me, and the stony silence that followed didn't help. "Can you turn up the radio?"

There was a buzz of energy and excitement at the pool. Each team had a designated area to sit and I shoved in close to my teammates. Colby was at the other end of the bench, mastering his Ignore Dori skills. I looked up at the observation deck and waved to Tor who was leaning up against the glass. He flashed me a wide grin and I melted a little bit. I wished I didn't have to put on my stupid swim cap. Along with the goggles I looked like a Martian. Vanity had to go out the window, though, if I wanted to win my heat.

The guys raced first. Colby lined up at his mark. My stomach clenched. I felt nervous for him. Despite all the weirdness between us, I still wanted the best for him.

The whistle blew and water splashed as the swimmers dove in. It was the butterfly heat, one of Colby's strongest swims. He easily took the lead. They headed back for the second lap, then a third and once the fourth and final lap was on, the noise of cheering in the pool area echoed to a deafening level. Our whole team was on its feet and I shouted the loudest.

Colby won by two arms lengths. Our team jumped and cheered and when Colby came back to our bench he gave me a big hug. (Huh!) He quickly moved on to high five the others. I glanced up at Tor. He raised his eyebrows in question with an amused look on his face. I shrugged and grinned back at him.

Everyone was buzzing about Colby's time. He'd broken the regional record.

"Awesome, Colby," I said. We managed to forget our differences for that brief happy moment.

My stomach flip-flopped when it was my turn to race. My heart beat in nervous anticipation—I depended on the adrenaline rush this produced to thrust me forward. I waited for the gun blast as I bent over the block.

I dove in and swam the butterfly hard. I didn't think of anything else except moving my arms and legs in a smooth rhythm. I wanted to win more than ever, just because Tor was here. I flipped at the end and moved onto my second length. Then my third. I could hear the din of the crowd through the water. One more lap. Knowing Tor was watching propelled me like never before. I knew I was making good time. I was sure I'd won.

I reached the end and tapped it with my hand. I was half a

pool length ahead of any of the other girls. I waited for the cheer the winners got, but instead all I got was a dull murmur.

Something was wrong.

People's heads were turned to the clock.

Not only had I beat my female competitors. I'd beat Colby's time. *I'd beat his time.* How did I beat his time?

Guys raced against guys because they were bigger, stronger and faster. It was nature. Men and women were built differently. I shouldn't have beaten a guy at this level of competition. And Colby had just broken a regional record.

I hopped out of the water. I looked up at Tor. What was he thinking? His arms were crossed and his eyes—worried? Perplexed? Or worse: *Disappointed?*

Colby was shouting at me when I got to the bench. "Cheater!"

"I'm not," I said, shocked. How quickly our camaraderie had deteriorated.

He yelled at Coach. "She's doing drugs. She has to be."

His eyes were a blaze of anger and humiliation.

I didn't think he meant to do what happened next. Maybe in his mind he wanted to, but he'd never really do it—I knew Colby, and I knew this. His arms were flailing wildly as he made his accusations. He meant to just point at me (I was sure of it), but instead he accidentally knocked me into the pool.

Of course I wasn't physically hurt, but it was just so shocking. To others it looked like I had just been attacked by my own teammate and Colby specifically. I pulled myself out wondering what all the sports columnists were going to write about us in the local papers now.

I felt shame and anger—I didn't do anything wrong. I snuck a sideways glance at Tor. His mouth was in a straight terse line. He pounded the glass with his fist. I'd bet he wished he could be down here to knock Colby's lights out, but the humidity forced him to stay away.

For once I was glad of it.

Mom's eyes were wide, her hand over her mouth. Dad had his arm around her shoulders, his brows furrowed.

Nana was gnawing on her lip, deep in thought. I didn't know what else she could be thinking about now. Maybe she really was losing her mind.

The swim meet officials conferred with Coach. He came back looking grim.

"They want to disqualify you, Dori. They say your time was impossible without enhancements. I convinced them to let your time stand until they can prove otherwise with drug testing."

"I'm clean," I whimpered.

"I'm afraid you're going to have to prove it."

The girls in the dressing room glared at me like I had leprosy, which with my red, itchy legs, wasn't too far off. Even Ally, who usually always smiled and accepted the fact that I was a stronger swimmer, didn't offer me a comforting glance.

I quickly rinsed off under the open stalled showers, swimsuit on, then wrapped my towel around myself.

Mom found me and threw her arms around me, no matter that I was wet and spotted her jacket. "We'll get to the bottom of this," she whispered.

A female judge walked in and called my name, *Elizabeth Seward*. Her voice resounded through the space like an echo chamber, and my first inclination was to run into a stall and hide.

Everyone else seemed confused—*Who's Elizabeth?* they whispered. They only knew me by my nickname. I stepped forward.

After asking my mother for permission she said to me,

"First let me take a blood sample, then you can pee in the cup." She handed me a plastic container, and I grew even redder with embarrassment. Would she like to strip-search me, too? I didn't think the female swim community was getting enough of a show here.

I sat on the bench as she took my hand and pricked my finger. Mom offered me her motherly comforting smiles. Then I trudged off to the toilets to fulfill the rest of my duties.

When we were finally able to leave I met up with the rest of my group in the foyer. My eyes were glossy and my face blotchy from holding back tears.

Dad patted me on the back and made soothing clucking noises. "It's not true," I pouted.

Nana reached for me next.

"This too shall pass," she said.

I stole a glimpse of Tor. He stood quietly to the side. I didn't know what to do. Go to him? Ignore him? I felt so embarrassed and humiliated; I just wanted to crawl into a hole and never come out.

Tor didn't know what to say either, apparently. The ride home was almost unbearable.

13

───────

I didn't sleep well. In my dreams I was at the pool, everyone's fingers pointing and jabbing my face. Then the scene changed and I was swimming with Tor, in the ocean. He kissed me, and then left. I swam after him, but he was so fast, and before I knew it, I couldn't see him. I was alone.

I woke with a start. Then I realized my cell phone was buzzing.

"Hello?" My voice was thick and groggy.

"Hi, it's me. Tor."

I already knew it was him by the call display. I was just surprised he was calling at all.

"I'm clean." Not what's up? Not how are you? Just, I'm clean. Would I forever be defending myself on this?

There was silence for a moment. Then Tor said, "Can we talk?"

"Okay." Might as well get this over with.

"Meet me at the beach in thirty minutes."

I had half an hour to get myself together. Thirty minutes to stew about what Tor wanted to talk about. I was pretty sure I knew. His uncle had gotten to him after yesterday's fiasco, and he wanted to end our friendship. Our relationship. Whatever it was that we were.

I washed my face with cold water and slathered cream on my legs. After last night's flare up, I was thinking stress might have something to do with it. I slipped on black, fitted athletic pants, a tank top and hoodie. I brushed my hair until it was smooth and pulled it back.

The last thing I could do was eat breakfast. My stomach was twisted up in a ball so tight, I couldn't fit a peanut in there. But I also didn't want to faint in front of Tor because of low blood sugar. I'd already suffered enough personal humiliation to last a lifetime. I drank a glass of orange juice and then brushed my teeth. Twenty minutes passed. I took a deep breath and headed out.

Tor was there when I arrived. He leaned against the rock, staring out at the bay. The sight of him took my breath away, and thinking about losing him so soon after I'd finally got him, felt like a slap in the face. I was still trying to shake off the emotional residue from my dreams. I swallowed hard and wrapped my arms around my stomach. *Hold it together, Dori.*

"Hey," he said when he saw me.

Instead of keeping his distance, he surprised me by rushing over and wrapping his arms around me. "You look like you could use a hug," he said.

That was all it took. I started sobbing like a baby. "I don't know what is wrong with me, Tor. I'm some kind of freak."

"Well, if you're a freak, I don't know what that makes me."

He kissed my forehead and I melted into him. Relief washed over me. This was not how a guy acted just before he was about to break up with you.

"I wanted to do this last night, but with your family all over you, I didn't want to intrude."

Oh, please, intrude away!

He took my hand and we climbed up on the rocks together. The sun peeked through the morning fog and I let the warmth of it calm me.

"I think I know what's going on with you."

"Really?" I was dying to know. "What?"

"You're going to think it's crazy."

"I already think I'm crazy."

"Remember when you asked me if a merperson has ever fallen in love with a human before?"

"Um, yes."

"I did some genealogy research of my kind last night. Apparently, it happened a couple generations ago. Here in Eastcove."

I shook my head. "I don't get it. What's that got to do with me?"

"I think you're one of us."

What? Stop the train. Did he just say what I thought he said? "Come again?"

"I think you are a descendant of that coupling. That's why you can swim beyond normal human abilities and hold your breath for so long."

"As much as I'd love to be a mermaid," I said without facetiousness. I'd been fantasizing about that ever since my awkward talk with Dex. "There seems to be one obvious flaw." I pointed to my legs. "No tail."

"Yet," he said softly. Then he reached up to my face. I thought he was about to pull me into a kiss when, instead he rubbed his hands behind my ears. Over the bumps!

I jerked away, mortified. I couldn't believe he'd just felt the acne behind my ears!

"I'm sorry, Dori," he said, noting my discomfiture. "I just had to check."

"Check for what?"

"Gill buds."

"What?"

"I've been suspicious for a while. Not that it makes any difference to how I feel about you. I was crazy about you when I thought you were fully human and now, with this, I'm ecstatic."

I was stuck for a moment on the "crazy about you" part, but then I got to the "with this" part.

"With what?"

"I noticed a while ago that your legs..."

Oh, my God. Was he going to pick out every physical flaw?

He continued, "... it's part of the process. I wasn't sure, because I've only witnessed it the other way around."

"Please, Tor. Speak English. I don't understand anything you're saying."

"You're fifteen. Not that that's a magic number, but it's around fifteen or sixteen that it happens."

"What happens?"

"Puberty. For merboys and mergirls."

I burst out laughing.

"It's true. I couldn't hop on a rock and form legs before puberty. Otherwise you'd see a lot of adventurous merchildren lying on rocks trying to get legs."

"Except that it's painful," I said. "That would be a deterrent."

"Yes, it would, I suppose."

"Okay, so with me?"

"Well, if you go the other way, from land to sea, the signs that your ability to shape shift is eminent are red, scaly legs and gill buds behind the ears."

I was strangely embarrassed, like I was discussing my

period with him or my need for a bra. "Wouldn't I have webbed fingers and toes?"

He chuckled. "Now *that's* a myth." Then he said, "Are you still bruising?"

"What do you mean?"

"I remember seeing you with a bruise on your shoulder."

"Yes, actually, I am. I think it's from running into my door jam on my way to the bathroom half asleep."

"Let me see."

I loosened my hoodie to reveal one shoulder. It was blue and green with swirly bruises. Tor gently rubbed his fingers along them and nervous electricity shot down my arm.

I breathed in deeply. "They're not real bruises are they?" Tor shook his head. "No, I don't think so."

I took a moment to let this news sink in. I went back to the part about a merfolk/human love affair happening before in Eastcove.

"Who was it?"

"What do you mean?"

I thought he knew but I spelled it out. "If I'm a mermaid, then someone in my genealogy, on my human side, fell in love with a merperson."

"Oh, yeah, that's true."

"So, spit it out, already, Tor. Who was it?"

"Your grandmother."

"You mean, like great-great-grandmother?"

Tor shook his head again.

I sucked in air. "Not Nana?"

"Yes."

"No. Way!"

I tried to picture this. Nana and Grandpa were married for thirty years, almost forever, before he died. I told this to Tor.

Tor ran his hands through his hair; clearly this conversation wasn't comfortable for him, either. "Your mother was a love child."

Suddenly, I found it hard to breathe. "You're making this up."

Tor locked his green eyes with mine. "Why would I do that?"

"I don't know. A sick joke."

"I wouldn't joke around about something like this."

"Okay, say I believe you. What you're saying is Nana had a fling with a merman, got pregnant by him, but married my grandfather and passed the kid off as his?"

Tor nodded carefully.

I felt sick, seriously. I'd never see Nana the same way again.

"So, how come my mother isn't a mermaid?"

"Same reason your brothers aren't merfolk. Why kids get their parent's eye color or don't. It's genetics. Actually, it's on both sides of your family."

"My father's, too?"

"Yeah, but farther back in the ancestry. Merfolk activity used to be quite high in these parts."

My heart beat so hard the blood swooshed in my ears, drowning out the roar of the ocean. Seagulls squawked and circled above and I wanted to run and chase them away. I wanted to throw something. Or maybe just throw up.

"Are you okay, Dori?"

"I'm not sure."

I jumped off the rocks and started walking. Tor was right behind me. He clasped my hand and stroked it with his thumb. It had a soothing effect.

"What do I do now?"

"About?"

"About becoming a mermaid, if I am even one, like you think."

"You need to swim. In the ocean. Not the pool. I think you need to quit swim club for a while. If it happened there, it would be catastrophic."

"I'm not exactly popular on my swim team at the moment." Not to mention that I was on temporary suspension until they cast a verdict. "I won't be showing up there for a while."

"Good." Tor squeezed my hand. "Everything is going to be fine."

I wished I could believe him.

THAT EVENING at dusk I stood, oh, so self-consciously, in front of Tor, in my bikini as per his recommendation. It wasn't fair since he was still fully dressed and unable to keep the smirk off his face. I had goose bumps on my goose bumps and somehow, even in the chill my legs were flaring red.

"I make a good lighthouse beacon," I said.

Tor laughed. "I think you're beautiful, and you better get in the water before I declare a change of plans."

I was nervous. It wasn't like I'd never gone swimming in the ocean before, even at dusk, but I'd never gone swimming with the intention of turning into a mermaid before. Especially with an audience.

I got my toes wet, and glanced back at Tor. He gave me an encouraging nod. We'd decided ahead of time that I would start off alone, with Tor watching from the shore. The plan was if I got in trouble with a current or rip tide, or, if *it* happened, he'd jump in. If he came in with me now, he wouldn't be able to come out with me if nothing happened.

The anticipation of entering mermaid-dom was causing an inner pillow fight, feathers flitting and flying everywhere throughout my nervous system.

"This is it!" I shouted back at Tor. I dove in, my breath

escaping as the chilly water encased my body. I popped my head out of the water and breathed, looking hopefully at Tor. I waited for the tingling sensation that Tor described to begin, but all I felt was the cold.

I swam, diving down, holding my breath as long as I could until my lungs were bursting. I watched my legs—they were still legs. Nothing happened.

When I tired out, I swam back to shore. Tor handed me a towel.

"I'm sorry," I said.

"You've got nothing to be sorry about."

"I don't know. Maybe I'm not a mermaid."

"Give it time."

"Tor?" I said as I rung out my hair. "What would I have done if I hadn't met you? If I'm really a mermaid, that is? What if I had changed in the pool? All your secrets would've been exposed."

"You wouldn't have changed if you hadn't met me. Or someone like me."

I stopped and thought about this. "*You're* changing me?"

"In a way. Association with me, with one of our kind, at the right time triggers the change."

"Hormones or something?"

Tor grinned.

Wow. I was turning because of some cosmic connection with Tor. If he was right and I actually turned, that was.

We walked back to my house, and Tor gave me a deliciously long and tasty kiss good night.

Nana was visiting again, sitting in the reclining chair by the living room window and my heart jumped a bit when I thought she might have spotted me kissing Tor. Mom sat across from her and they were both cradling a cup of tea.

"Were you swimming?" Mom said. "It's dark."

"It's summer, and it only just got dark," I said. I offered Nana the slimmest greeting I could get away with, and headed to the kitchen to make myself a snack. Cereal sounded quick and easy. I just wanted to escape upstairs to my room before Mom tried to pull me into a cozy girls' night.

I could barely look at Nana now that I knew her secret. First of all, I found it hard to believe that Nana would do something like that. Not just have an affair when she was with Grandpa, but continue to let my mom think that he was her biological father.

Tor couldn't say who her biological father really was.

And the way she was sitting there, across from my mother, making small talk and girl-bonding, all with that GREAT BIG SECRET sitting in the room with them, it made me want to barf.

If it was all even true. Maybe I was being totally unfair. I hadn't turned into a mermaid yet and this whole story about Nana could be a big mistake—I'd probably end up laughing it off sometime in the near future and we'd go on like before. Like normal.

I slurped the milk at the bottom of my bowl.

When I put my bowl on the floor for Crosby to lick up the remaining milk, it dawned on me. Maybe Nana suspected something. That was why she kept staring at Tor like she was trying to decipher a code.

That was what she meant when she told me I could tell her anything. She wanted me to confide in her about him.

How much did Nana really know about the merfolk world? Did she go swimming with her merman the way I have with Tor?

Probably. For some reason this thought made me gag. No one liked to think of their parents getting intimate, much less their grandmother with a merman.

Like anything would ever be normal again. Nana might have her secrets but I had mine, too.

My dreams that night were lucid. I was swimming joyfully, underwater, doing somersaults like a little kid. I never felt panic about drowning. I didn't have a tail, but I could breathe. Tor was in them, too. We swam together, effortlessly. The funny thing was, he didn't have a tail, either. He had legs.

14

*C*rowd had gathered at the boardwalk when I arrived for work. I couldn't tell at first who was causing the commotion, and then I saw Crazy Jim's greasy head. He wore layers of drab clothing that hadn't been washed in eons. I could see the gap in his teeth a mile away.

"I swear to you that I saw her again, early this morning, I did." His growly bass-like voice spread across the beach. "She has long red hair and a tail. We have our own mermaid, folks, right here in the Bay of Fundy!"

I moaned.

"I think he really believes it," Becca said.

Samara tut-tut-ed. "He's delusional. They may have to lock him up soon."

I bit my lip, listening as Crazy Jim went on and on. *Shut up, already.*

"I'll prove it!" he shouted when the crowd mocked and laughed at him. "I'll prove it, I swear. I'll catch'er in my net and bring her to this very beach. I will, mark my words. Then we'll see who's laughing." Crazy Jim marched away with a determined scowl on his weather-beaten face.

I didn't doubt he'd make good on his threats for a minute. I had to let Tor know they had a merfolk hunter on their hands.

"Excuse me." I took off before Becca or Samara could object, and raced to the other end of the boardwalk to Tor's kiosk. If he'd been there, he would've heard Crazy Jim's proclamations himself, but it was empty.

A dark sense of foreboding blanketed me and I rushed down the beach in the direction of Tor's cave.

The problem was, I'd only been there a couple of times and Tor always led the way. I wasn't sure how to find it.

I climbed rocks and pushed through forest bramble where it interfaced. I scoured the landscape for something that seemed familiar, a landmark of some kind, but drew a blank.

Tor and Dex knew what they were doing when they chose a spot that no one else would stumble upon.

I was thirsty and worn out, but my desperate need to see Tor again pushed me on. It had to be around here somewhere. Then I spotted the crack in the rocks. The slim crevice that I'd needed Tor's help to get down.

I reached blindly for purchase with my foot. I managed to grip a ledge with my toe but then was at a loss as to where to place my hands. I gripped the edge tenuously, groping one hand at a time until I caught something to grab. The descent was precarious, and I missed the bottom by a foot and crashed to the sandy floor.

I moaned, examining my ankle, but, except for scratches and (real) bruising, everything checked out.

I crept up the rock precipice to the opening of their cave. It was dark. The lanterns were out. Fear taunted me; I was too late, they'd left.

I couldn't believe that Tor would leave without me. Or, at least, that he would leave without saying goodbye.

"Tor?" I called out. "Are you here?"

"Dori?" Tor's silhouette appeared in the semi darkness, and relief washed over me. He took a moment to light a lantern. I could see his face, pinched with worry.

"Crazy Jim is telling everyone he saw a mermaid. Again."

"I know."

"Well, did he? Was it Shava?" I climbed up the steps and Tor stepped aside as I entered the cave.

"I'm afraid so." He touched my lower back and guided me through the dimness.

"Why is she being so careless?" We'd never even met and I wanted to ring her neck.

A baritone voice called out, "She's jealous." Dex appeared out of the shadows. "Of you."

I looked at Tor. "I thought you said she was a cousin?"

"She is."

"Then why would she be jealous of me?"

Dex answered for him, "Our world is small. Cousins mate all the time."

My head swiveled back to Tor. "She wants to mate with you?" I wanted to vomit on the word "mate."

"It's a long story," he said with a sigh. I bet it was.

After my eyes adjusted, I saw that the laptop was opened, and a pile of maps and books were lying on the table and over the floor.

"What's going on?" I said. "You're not leaving because of this? No one believes anything Crazy Jim says. It'll be an old story in a few days."

"They don't believe him yet, but if we don't deal with Shava, they will. It's not just your Crazy Jim we have to worry about. We have troubles of our own."

"What do you mean?"

Tor hesitated. "I can't really get into it right now. Just that there's tension in the merfolk world. We have to help keep peace."

We were interrupted by a gentle musical clicking, much like what I had witnessed coming from Tor before.

"What's that?"

"Uncle Dex."

That was when I noticed that he was no longer in the room with us. "What's he doing?"

"He's talking with our folk."

I doubled back to the maps on the floor, maps of the ocean, and realized now what Tor and Dex were doing. Plotting defensive strategy.

"Are you leaving?" I said, my throat catching.

"Not yet."

Not yet.

I glanced at my watch and noted the time. I'd been gone from the fruit stand too long. Becca was going to have a conniption. "I've got to go, but you'll still be here tonight?"

Tor stood with me. "Yes, I wouldn't leave without letting you know." He took my hand. "I'll walk you back."

That was good, because I could use help climbing that rock wall to get out of here. And I wanted as much time with Tor now as possible.

"Where'd you run off to?" Becca said as I jogged back. She was sneaking berries from a bowl she'd stashed under the counter.

"I just wanted to say hi to Tor."

"That was a long hello," she said with a conspirator's smile.

I shrugged and grinned back at her, hoping she wouldn't catch how fake it felt. "Well, you know?"

"Good thing it hasn't been busy."

"Yeah, sorry. I'll try to control myself next time."

Mentally, I was far away from the fruit stand, hardly aware of the tourists walking the boardwalk. I rang in customers by habit.

"Dori? What's with you today?" Becca said. "You are out in la-la land."

"Uh, sorry, just daydreaming."

I was wracking my brain for a way to keep the *not yet* from happening.

15

Mom came into the kitchen with a stack of envelopes the next morning while I ate breakfast. "Mail call," she said, then handed me a letter.

I was surprised at first because I never got any mail. I mean, who would write to me when there was email?

My hands shook when I saw who it was from. The Maritimes Swimming Association. The verdict was inside. Was I guilty or innocent? I ripped it open.

Dear Ms Seward,

The results of your tests have been forwarded to us. We are please to advise you that you have been cleared of any possible drug enhancement use, and are officially re-instated to the Provincial Swim Team.

Sincerely,

John Brewster

President.

. . .

I SHOWED the letter to Mom.

"This is terrific, Dori." She gave me a big hug. "Of course, I knew you were innocent, but it's so great to get your name cleared. You must be so relieved."

I shrugged. "I'm not going back."

"Dori, I know it was embarrassing but you can't let this little incident stop you from pursuing your dreams. You know, get back on the horse, and all that."

How could it be my dream anymore when I was hampered by a possible mermaid transformation?

Unless I wasn't. Maybe I shouldn't make any rash decisions.

"I'll think about it," I said, stuffing the letter in my back pocket. "Anyway, I gotta run. I'm going sailing this morning. Dad said it was okay."

"I'm not crazy about you going out alone, Dori."

"It's a beautiful day. I just need time to clear my head. I won't be long. I've got my cell phone with me if I have any problems, which I won't."

IT TURNED out I wasn't the only one with plans to go out on this perfect summer day. Colby and Tiffany were at the docks, too. I could hear her giggle and felt them staring.

I stared right back at them.

"Seaweed!" Colby called out. "Where's your boyfriend?"

I ignored him. Not his business.

"He probably dumped her, Colby," Tiffany said just loud enough for me to hear. "No one wants to date a cheater."

That was it. I stomped over to them, relishing Tiffany's shocked expression and flipped out the letter from my back pocket.

"I didn't cheat," I said, waving it in their faces. Colby

plucked it from my hand, his eyes narrowing as they scanned left to right. I considered telling him that he probably didn't have to worry about competing next to me anymore, because I'd likely be quitting swim team, but decided to keep that info to myself a little longer. Let him sweat it out a bit.

I didn't wait for a response, because, quite frankly, I didn't care what they thought. I snatched my letter back and turned on my heels without another word.

I did my pre-sail check, started the motor, and putted out of the marina. I liked to sail when I was stressed and with everything going on with Tor, I felt stressed. Running into Colby and Tiffany didn't help.

I headed out farther than I usually go, the sails rippling in the wind. I breathed in deeply, letting the sun caress my face. The farther I got from shore the more I relaxed. I let myself become one with the boat, skimming the waves.

Sometimes the sails mask the view, like a blind spot. You had to be careful that they didn't shield the sight of oncoming marine traffic.

Usually, I was extremely cautious, fully aware of my surroundings. I guess I could blame stress, or the fact I hadn't been sleeping that well, but mostly, I just had to take the blame. I wasn't being careful enough.

I'd let my eyes close for just a second. Just a second, I swore. I was jerked off balance by a big thunk and a sickening crunch. I ducked in time to miss getting my head chopped off by the main sail boom as it whipped over my head.

Water rushed into my small craft, swallowing it. I flapped my arms, waves gushing over my head and up my nose. In my peripheral I caught sight of another larger vessel.

My heart beat in panic as I realized I'd been hit. Our family boat was destroyed and it was my fault!

And I hadn't put on a life jacket. I never did. I was an

expert swimmer.

I recognized the weather beaten fishing boat. It belonged to Crazy Jim. I cried out for help because the shore was too far away, even for me to make it.

My cries for help were masked by the wind and jumping waves. I felt something tangle in my feet.

Crazy Jim's fishing net.

It dragged me under. I struggled with the ropes, panic loud in my chest like the beating of a native drum.

I was pulled deeper and deeper, the light of the sun shining through the water fading.

My lungs burned.

I kicked my feet like mad, trying to break loose from the net. I'd been sucked under the surface for too long. Longer than I'd ever held my breath before.

I managed to get my feet free, but it was too late. I was too far down to get to the surface on time.

This was it? This was how I die?

It all happened so fast. I waited for my life to flash before my eyes with a saint of some sort beckoning me to traverse down a tunnel of light.

Then, oddly, the burning in my chest subsided. A strange waving sensation tickled my ears. I touched them.

My pimples were soft and feathery, exuding bubbles.

Gills!

My legs felt tingly, and even though I was half expecting it, it still stunned me. I looked like Tor.

16

*A*ck!!!!!

A freaking tail! I no longer had legs. My mind still wanted to work two appendages; do the splits, anything, but it was like having only one leg. One very strong muscular leg.

I felt myself hyperventilating through the gills behind my ears, blinding myself with bubbles. My chest didn't expand but I could tell my heart still worked. The beating pounded loudly in my head until I thought it would just pop off.

I closed my eyes and imagined myself in my bed. *This is a dream, Dori. Take a deep breath and calm down.*

I faked myself out like that for a while, warm and floating, wanting to believe I would wake up any minute with my legs intact, knowing that I was immersed in water and what Tor had told me about myself was true.

I was a mermaid.

This was what I'd wanted, right? *So, stop freaking out.* I opened my eyes. I'd been underwater for over ten minutes. I hadn't drowned. I wasn't dead and I wasn't dying. I could do this.

White debris on the ocean floor caught my eye. A lump formed in my throat as I watched the last pieces of my sailboat settle in the silt. I had no idea how I was going to explain the accident to my family.

When I took in my surroundings, I realized I could see better than usual. Instead of my vision being gray and cloudy like it normally was when I swam without goggles, the undersea world around me was oddly vivid, like an artist's rendering in HD. The blue/green of the water shimmered like a jewel. Around me the cod and flounder were almost neon, and the ocean floor moved like a fluid carpet.

I was still processing that I was breathing under water— with gills.

And, yes, I had my own spectacular tail. I instinctively knew how to work it. Now that I'd stopped freaking out completely, I tested it with a couple underwater loopdy-loops.

I wasn't sure what it looked like to all my new underwater buddies, but I didn't blame them one bit for skittering away as fast as they could. I flapped my arms, spinning in circles, my long hair floating glamorously around my head, a wispy flag of white-blond in surrender. I gave in to my exhaustion and floated like a piece of dead driftwood, letting the current take me where it willed.

I dazed out in some kind of burned out I-can't-freaking-believe-this-actually-happened coma state when I heard the song of the northern right whale. That was when I noticed how fine-tuned my hearing was—I felt like a human radio receiver.

I righted myself into a vertical position, startled by the nearness of the whale as she moseyed on by. Her impressive stocky body, with her square-ish head and bumpy skin, was so close I could reach out and touch her. Her dark eyes took me in with amusement but I wasn't (very) afraid. She'd seen my kind before. I knew she fed on zooplankton, but I would've been a fool not to respect her, and so I kept my distance.

I watched the northern right until it was out of sight. I found my heart rate had finally slowed and I focused on my gills until my breaths calmed. I twirled around ballerina style, momentarily losing myself, totally into the freedom I was now enjoying underwater. I found myself dancing in new-found giddy joy with my recent mermaid-ness. Laughing underwater produced a wave of happy bubbles, which made me want to laugh even more.

Then I finally snapped out of my world of awe.

I needed to find Tor and tell him that he was right. I was a *mermaid*. The strangest thing was, I *knew* how to find him. Instinct was awesome!

I shut off my mind to logic and just swam, allowing myself to rise to just below the surface. It took a while, but eventually I neared the cove. For the first time since I'd gotten my gills, I surfaced, sticking my face above the water. I didn't know what I'd expected, but I sucked in air and my lungs kicked in like normal.

I had to know; could I still breathe underwater, then? I dipped my head under and held my breath. Within seconds my gills activated.

Once I stopped playing, lungs/gills/lungs/gills, I refocused on the task at hand. Find Tor. I saw the tall dark jagged rocks near shore with an almost invisible vertical crevice in the middle. The tide was low and I was thankful there was still enough water in the bay to get me to the cave entrance.

Also, because the tide was low, the rock Tor had used to hoist himself out of the water was out of reach. There were several more flat, human-sized rocks at various levels, and I had a feeling that it wasn't accidental. Tor and his uncle had worked hard to make this cave work. We just had to keep its existence from discovery.

I hopped on the rock, and for the first time got a full out-of-water view of my new body. I had to admit that my tail was a beautiful, deep seaweed green, with glistening pinks, blues and purples swirling throughout.

I still wore my long tank top, but I could see the tattoo-like markings that now covered both of my shoulders and part way down my biceps. I wasn't sure how I'd explain those to my parents.

I gasped with the first jolt of pain. Oh, yeah, the painful tail-to-leg part. Ow—another jolt, stronger this time; I cried out for Tor.

More knife-like searing. This must be what it felt like to be shot with a Taser gun, or subjected to some kind of ancient torture, like when they pulled on your legs and squeezed you in a compressor at the same time.

I heard myself wailing, tears falling off my face onto the drying rock.

"Tor!"

"Dori?"

I cried out again. "Tor? Help?"

Instead of coming to my side, Tor disappeared. I breathed deeply through my nose and out slowly through my mouth, like you see those women do on TV when they're in labor.

Tor came back with a blanket. He lay down beside me, covering my tail. I didn't know why he did that. It wasn't like I was cold. Then I remembered the satellites.

Another jab of pain. I sobbed into Tor's shoulder.

He stroked my hair. "It'll be over soon."

I held onto his chest hoping he was right. One last stab, less intense than the others and then it was over.

I lifted the blanket to check. The tail was gone. I had legs. I was also naked. I assumed my shorts were shredded and lying at the bottom of the ocean.

"Dori, are you all right?"

I was breathing through my lungs now, obviously, but I panted like a dog. I feared I would succumb to shock.

"I don't know," I said weakly.

Tor wrapped the blanket around me, taking in my tattoos, and checking out the back of my ears.

"I told you not to swim alone," he said, but I didn't have a chance to defend myself. Tor swooped me into his arms and climbed the rocks back to the caves.

It was in that strange moment—with Tor's strong arms around my limp body, my hair dripping in wild, clumpy strands down my back, hanging on the best I could to his neck as he deftly climbed the rocks—that I thought I might be in love.

17

ore than anything else in the world I needed to make a way for him to stay. This was my only mission. Tor and I were meant for each other, I was sure of it. Who else could I share this underworld experience with? Who else could know the pain of transforming a tail into legs?

Tor gently laid me down on the cot. I locked in on his emerald eyes, wondering if he was feeling the same thing. Did he love me, too?

Dex cleared his throat, fracturing the magic of the moment. Tor and I broke our gaze and turned to him. He raised a bushy eyebrow.

"I was right," Tor said.

Dex got busy making tea while Tor brought me a pair of his sweatpants and T-shirt. They'd be baggy but I was thankful. He pointed to the bathroom.

It was a smaller, cave-like room carved out in the back of the main cave. Inside was a camper toilet and sink with water that you pumped through the system with your foot. A mirror hung from the rock face.

I couldn't help but deeply breathe in the scent of Tor as I pulled his shirt over my head. It covered my tattoos and my butt, but wasn't long enough to be a T-shirt dress. I pulled on the sweats and rolled them up to mid calf.

Then I looked in the mirror and groaned. Not exactly drop-dead-gorgeous happening here.

There was a brush on the narrow counter and I borrowed it, wincing as I tugged through the tangles. I pulled the loose hair out of the brush and tossed it into the garbage can before leaving the brush on the counter and returning to Tor and Dex.

Uncle Dex set a cup of hot tea on the table in front of me and I drank it gratefully. Though I'd never once felt cold the whole time I was in the ocean, now I shivered. Tor left and came back with a hoodie. At this rate, the guy wouldn't have anything left to wear himself.

Tor wanted answers. "What happened?"

"I was sailing. It's what I like to do when I need to think. I had everything in control, just skimming along when I was hit."

"You were hit?"

"Yeah, Crazy Jim, can you believe it? He's on a quest to find a mermaid and he didn't even see my boat! Or me for that matter when I called for help."

"So, what happened?"

"My feet got tangled up in his fishing net and I got pulled under."

"And..."

"I would've drowned, if I wasn't...this."

Tor's eye's narrowed and his face grew dark. "I'm so sorry, Dori."

"Why? It's not your fault."

Dex cleared his throat. "Your, uh, Crazy Jim, is looking for us?"

"Yeah, but he's crazy. No one believes his stories."

"He believes them. Besides, we have a policy of clearing out of any area where humans have inadvertently spotted us. We've already broken the rule with the first sighting."

No. I felt panic rising.

Tor and Dex stared at each other like they were talking without using words.

We can't wait any longer. We have to leave now.

Yes, I know, you're right. But what about her?

What about me? And why did I know what they're thinking? "I can hear you," I blurted. "I know you're not talking but I hear you, and I'm coming."

Dex sat back with wide eyes. "She really is one of us,"

"Dori," Tor said, running his hands through his hair. "The best thing for you to do is to just go home. Be with your family."

"But what if I don't want to do the best thing. What if I want to be with you?"

A soft smile formed on Tor's face. "Believe me, there's nothing more I want right now than to be wherever you are, but things aren't quite...settled at home."

"Since when is it your decision?" I folded my arms stubbornly in front of my chest. I could feel my heart beating rapidly, my mind skipping back over the part where Tor just said he wanted to be with me more than anything.

The logical part of my brain was saying that Tor was right, I should stay. Think about my family.

But my heart was anything but logical right now.

Tor's lips tugged downward. I thought he knew me well enough to know I could be pretty stubborn. He handed me his cell phone.

"Call your mother," he said.

I took the phone but didn't dial. Instead I noticed for the first time how sparse the room was.

"We have to leave," Tor said, seeing my eyes scan the place. "At least for a while."

"Where to?"

Tor and Dex exchanged a look before Dex answered. "The world's oceans are vast. Even though humans have managed to map large portions, they haven't found everything there is to find."

"And?" I prompted.

Tor jumped in. "Just like on earth, there are mountain ranges under the sea. Caves and cliffs. We're transient sea dwellers; we're always moving around, from place to place."

I smiled. "Ah, like undersea gypsies. But I thought you had to stay coastal, to, you know, breathe air sometimes."

"Only the ones like Uncle Dex and me who want to live partially on land. The others never have to surface, so they can live anywhere there are caves and mountains to hide in. Even so, we can stay underwater for weeks at a time."

Up to now, I'd only envisioned Dex and Tor and a nuclear family. "How many of you are there, exactly?"

"More than you'd think. There are two main clans, but each clan has many pods."

I was dumbfounded. "Tell me about the clans."

Tor hesitated. "It's a long story. We don't really have time to get into it now." He nodded to the phone. "Call your mother, and then I'll walk you home."

I walked up the rock steps to the outdoors, Tor on my heels. I called my mother, but I didn't tell her about destroying the boat, or that I was on my way home. I told her I was spending the weekend with Becca on her farm after work.

Tor's expression was grim. "What are you doing?"

"I'm going with you. I'm a mermaid now, and I want to go meet the clan."

"Dori." Tor grimaced. "That's a dumb idea."

"Why? It's not like I'd be gone forever. You said so yourself."

I followed Tor back into the cave. He told Dex what I'd done.

Dex cleared his throat. "It's dangerous, Dori. Tor's right, you should stay here and wait for us to come back."

"What's so dangerous about it?"

Tor and Dex stared each other down.

She's exactly what they want. Once their spies spot her, it'll be trouble. Dex said.

I don't think we can stop her. And you can't blame her for being curious. Let's just show her around the pod, and then I'll bring her back myself.

I didn't know if they'd forgotten that I could hear them, but I didn't let on. I registered Dex's concern and made a mental note to ask Tor later on about who *they* were and why they had spies.

One day, then you bring her back.

One day.

One day—I scoffed with my inside voice, but I'd let them think what they want for now. I smiled at my victory.

"Okay." Tor stood and I stood, too.

Dex waved us off. "I'll deal with the rest of this stuff and join you later."

"What are you doing with it?" I asked.

"Uncle Dex rented a storage unit." Tor tilted his head. "Let's go."

Let's go. This was it. Little tingling shivers shot throughout my body. I was going to some foreign place under the sea. With Tor.

All my fears melted away when Tor took my hand. Suddenly, irrationally, all was right with the world.

Down at the rocks, Tor paused. "Are you sure you're ready for this?"

That was when I clued in that we were going to become merpeople—a mercouple—for the first time.

I nodded. Tor took off his shirt and my innards quaked.

"I don't like to swim with clothes on," he explained at my startled look. "It's just not a natural feeling."

"Well, um, I'm keeping my shirt, well, your shirt on, if you don't mind."

He smirked. "I can go either way. But I'll warn you, it's way more comfortable to transition without pants on."

I could feel my eyes blinking madly.

"I'm taking mine off."

"Oh, oh, all right." I turned around, horribly embarrassed. I couldn't believe this situation never crossed my mind. And what about me? I'd have to remove his sweatpants. I blushed with modesty. I had brothers, but even they had never seen me naked. It just wasn't the way we did things at home.

I heard a splash, and I figured it was safe to turn around. Tor's clothes were tucked away between the rocks. His head bobbed up and he flashed his adorable grin. "Your turn."

"Turn around," I instructed.

"I'll do better than that. I'll submerge. I'll wait for you underneath."

"But you can still see me underwater!" I remembered how advanced my vision was as a mermaid.

He laughed. "Fine, I'll turn around underwater."

I couldn't believe how nervous I was. I slipped off the sweatpants and hoodie, stretching Tor's T-shirt down as far as possible, even though I knew no one could see me. Except the space satellites, maybe. The thought of that freaked me out and I quickly slipped into the ocean.

I braced myself for pain, but was pleasantly surprised with

nothing more than spurts of tingling, like when you sit on your foot and it falls asleep. Much like the first time. Not entirely comfortable, but bearable. My legs stiffened up and fused together, forming my tail. It happened in minutes and before I knew it I was submerged, flicking my tail around and swirling through the water. My gills immediately began functioning, not even a moment of stress with breathing.

Nothing felt more natural. I belonged in the ocean.

And then I saw Tor.

I gasped. Or at least, my mouth dropped open and bubbles came out.

His tattoos swirled in brilliant blues and purples, reflective of his tail.

His tail.

My tail.

We had tails. I still couldn't comprehend it. Tor swam over to me, his grin wide, tiny bubbles escaping from behind his ears. His eyes were a brilliant green, and he peered into mine.

I've dreamed about this day.

Me too.

I didn't have time to think about the fact that we'd just spoke to each other without talking.

He stroked strands of hair away from my face, holding on to the nape of my neck. He wrapped his tail around mine.

I thought I would die of happiness. If anything happened to float by and touch us, we'd kill it, too, I was sure.

Tor leaned in, and his lips touched mine. I shivered and quivered, but he didn't seem to mind. His lips were warm and soft even under water. I was lost in his kisses. For this moment in time it was just me and Tor.

We swam off, diving deeper. I had no idea where we were going. Or when I'd come back.

18

*T*he tone of the water had changed to a deeper, darker blue. I was aware of sounds and sensations I'd never experienced before. Sonar waves from deep-sea life, patterns in the currents, the roar of motors from boats overhead.

And I realized I didn't know where I was.

Of course, I didn't know where I was. I was swimming far under the surface in the middle of the Atlantic Ocean, propelling myself with a *tail*. I'd hardly been out of Eastcove, much less to some foreign destination under the sea. I felt a little distressed and I squeezed Tor's hand harder.

He turned back and smiled, oblivious to my growing irrational fears. Like people who were afraid of heights, was I afraid of depths?

Yet, I couldn't deny the call of the ocean, and when I thought of returning to land, especially without Tor, well, that sort of anxiety was greater.

Even though I felt bad about lying to my mom, I knew I'd made the right decision. I needed to know more about Tor, his family and his world.

My world now.

Plus, I couldn't face being without Tor. Again, I was amazed at how fast this had happened, like an inner switch flicked on without asking. I mentally recited all the things I liked about him: of course, he was gorgeous, but also strong—I felt safe with him; he was thoughtful, he got my jokes, he made me feel special. I could be myself around him.

My true self. Now that I was merfolk, no ordinary boy would ever do. I was ruined.

As he led me confidently to wherever we were headed, I was overwhelmed with the strength of my feelings for him.

Wait, could he *hear* what I was thinking? I felt my face flush red, even in the water. How exactly did this talking without speaking thing actually work? I wished I would've asked Tor more questions about it when I could still use my vocal chords.

I noticed him glancing back at me. His lips pulled up in a tender grin.

Because he heard me *think*? Did that mean none of my thoughts were private anymore? This was definitely problematic, because I never stopped thinking and mostly, lately, I thought about Tor. Not good.

But, I couldn't hear Tor think. Was it because he knew how to control his thoughts? How to keep his mind blank? I'd heard this was a skill that guys had. Or, what? I decided I had to try it out right now. This couldn't wait.

Tor?

Yeah?

I was so stunned, I pulled up short, my hand slipping out of his. Tor hovered in front of me, concern on his face. *Are you okay?*

Do you hear everything I think?

That's what's wrong?

Just answer the question?

He smiled sheepishly. *Not everything.*

What do you mean, not everything? How does this think-speak work?

He chuckled and I wanted to kick him. Which was difficult when you didn't have legs.

When you want to say something to someone, you address that person, or that group with your mind. Then everything you say after that is transmitted to them.

You mean, I just have to think about that person, and he can hear me?

His eyes sparkled and I could tell he was trying to hold in laughter. *You may need to work on your communication transmission skills.*

I punched him in the arm (which was highly ineffective underwater) and he swam away, laughter bubbles escaping from his gills.

I was officially a mortified mermaid.

My mental agony worked well at helping to pass the time. I reviewed everything I'd thought over in my mind, wondering what it was that Tor could've "heard" and then realized he was probably listening in right *now*. This was a vicious circle. I didn't really notice the vast mass of liquid blue all around me, or the creatures that blended in and out.

Tor's voice drew me from my misery. *We're here.* He pointed to a network of underwater caves in an undersea mountain range. My jaw dropped as I gawked at it in awe. I'd never even seen mountains on land. Not real mountains like the Rockies, and I'd bet these underwater mountains could challenge them in mass and splendor.

We dove deeper, through the pinks and purples of cold water coral. I confessed to being more than a little unnerved by a distant encounter with a school of pointy-nosed spiny dogfish sharks with their odd cat-like whiskers They weren't large, only a meter long, but traveled in intimidating packs. Tor circled wide when we spotted them.

Tor made that clicking sound I'd heard him make on the first day I'd seen him. Except that I heard it in my head rather than with my ears. I guessed he was announcing our arrival.

I couldn't tell where exactly we were headed, but soon a dark speck on the side of a mountain grew larger until I could see that it was the opening of a cave. We paused along a nearby ridge. Two large, solid looking mermen hovered along either side of the cave opening. It was weird to see another merperson other than Tor. Tor's eyes moved from one to the other, and there seemed to be some kind of communication going on, though I couldn't hear anything

Who's that?

Tor didn't respond. Then I remembered I had to address him.

Tor?

Before he could answer me, we were joined by a merfolk couple that had to be his parents.

Like most reunions when the son came home from a faraway journey, his mother greeted him with much emotion. She was a flamboyant, beautiful mermaid with porcelain skin and thick wavy auburn hair. Her upper body was (thankfully) covered with mounds of necklaces, sparkling jewels and pearls strung together; I could only guess where they'd come from. Her tail was a lighter shade of green, almost pinkish.

She had Tor in a strong embrace, moving her head from side to side, touching both of Tor's cheeks. I waited for her verbal burst of joy, but then realized, to my dismay, that I couldn't hear what they were saying to each other, and they were clearly communicating. Obviously they hadn't *addressed* me. In fact, she barely gave me a sideways glance.

Tor's mother was followed by a massive merman with huge bulky biceps, his entire torso covered in extraordinary tattoos. His bushy black hair reached midway down his back, and his face was almost hidden with facial hair. His eyes were deep pools of emerald green—like Tor's—and they were fixed on his son.

Again they spoke and I couldn't hear. I felt like the deaf guest at an all-hearing affair.

I awkwardly stayed off to the side, waiting for an introduction. I got the feeling they hadn't expected their son to bring a girl home.

Just when I thought the introductions were finally forthcoming, two more merpeople swam to Tor. The first one was a younger merman who greatly resembled Tor, though bigger and older. I gathered this was Tor's brother. Missing was the familial warmth that had come from Tor's parents. They shared a congenial handshake and quick parting.

The second creature was female, petite, pretty with flaming red hair. A mini alarm went off in my head. She, too, had a collection of exotic necklaces that covered her chest. I glanced down at the T-shirt I wore, all stretched out from the weight of the water, and suddenly I felt like the ugly girl at the dance who was pitifully under-dressed.

When I looked up, the redhead was lip-locked in a kiss with Tor. If I'd had knees they would be buckling. As it was I felt like someone was plugging up my gills, and I vacillated between wanting to faint and disappear and wanting to tackle that mergirl to the seafloor.

Hello! Tor!

To his credit, he did look like he was trying to pull away from her, but obviously not hard enough. I was ticked off. This whole thing reeked of rudeness and something else I was afraid to find out about. Like, who was this mergirl, (though I had a sick feeling that I knew) and why did Tor just let her kiss him like that?

Tor swam over to my side and drew me in to this sicko love fest.

This is my friend, Dori of Eastcove. Awkward silence. I could only fixate on his choice of words. FRIEND. His family squinted and stared at me and my T-shirt like they didn't know what to think or say. As if Tor had just brought home a beluga whale or a sea turtle and wanted to know if he could keep it as a pet.

Dori, this is my mother, Queen Alia, and my father, King Playo.

What? Queen and king? He never told me that? And did that make Tor a prince? I didn't have time to process this information as each of them took my hand and shook it.

Hello, I said not sure if they could hear me, and wondering if I was supposed to perform some kind of tail curtsy, with them being royalty.

Welcome to our clan, Tor's mother said. *At least the small part represented here today.*

Thank you.

We are glad to make your acquaintance, King Playo said.

Tor continued, *Over here is my brother, Kon.* Kon gave me a polite wave, though I didn't hear any words. But if I could read anything from his expression, he wasn't entirely happy to meet me.

And this is Shava.

Freak, I knew it. The redhead who started all the trouble in the first place.

Shava swam over to me and did this delicate mermaid curtsy (so now I knew). I didn't hear her say anything, so I just mimicked her move (poorly) and offered a weak smile.

I was afraid to think anything, because as Tor said, I didn't quite have a handle on my communication transmission skills. I was afraid they were all going to hear how uncomfortable I was with these introductions and how angry I was about that kiss.

Queen Alia motioned us to go inside the cave. Close up, I got a better look at the two oversized mermen that waited on either side of the door. They had bulky muscular arms crossed over defined pectoral muscles. Unlike Tor and his family, these two mermen had leather belts around their waists, each with a knife sheath with a bone handle sticking out.

I questioned Tor with my eyes.

My parent's royal sentinels. Bodyguards.

Like caves inhabited by transient dwellers above the ground, these caves were sparse in décor. It wasn't like you could hang a picture or throw a rug under water. Plus it was dark. Obviously, no oil lamps to shed light. I felt Tor's hand on my arm and I wondered if I was the only one who couldn't see anything. Great. Now I was deaf and blind. My chest tightened with frustration and anger and something else. I wanted air. My lungs were starting to rebel. I wasn't used to not using them. In the blackness, I felt kind of panicky and I grabbed on to Tor more tightly than usual.

Are you okay?

I don't know. I can't see. I can't hear. And I'm finding it hard to breathe. What do you think?

Dori, you're worked up. Just relax. Focus on your gills. Your eyes will adjust in time.

I found his neck with my chin and nuzzled in. I focused on my gills taking in oxygen and on the strength of Tor's body next to mine.

He was right. My eyes began to adjust, like someone had plugged in a night light. Two feet ahead of me was Shava's face.

I startled backward. *What's the matter with her?*

Shava, Tor said gently, *you need to give us some space, okay? Dori's a guest.*

Shava's eyes said it all. She was heartbroken.

Tor? I turned from Shava and tried to whisper with my think-speaking, not sure if Shava could hear me or not. *You said you were cousins.*

Tor moved us to the far side of the cave, away from Shava and all the members of his family. *We are cousins.*

Then I remembered what Dex had said about their small world and cousins mating. *Are you two an item?*

Tor looked away, clearly uncomfortable. Then he met my eyes. *We were. We're not anymore.*

Are you sure? She doesn't seem to agree.

It's really hard for Shava. If I hadn't decided to go ashore, we'd still be together. But I made my choice. I can't be with someone I'll have to leave all the time.

Obviously, she doesn't agree with your choice. Is that why she surfaced in the bay? Did she mean to get spotted?

Yes, she came to the bay to find me, but she didn't mean to be spotted. She's a gentle soul and would never purposely cause anyone any harm.

I folded my arms. I hated how he sided with her. And I didn't believe for a second that she didn't mean to be spotted. A slithery coil of jealously wrapped around my heart. Tor was mine now, and I was going to make sure that Gentle Shava knew that.

19

———

Queen Alia swam over to my side. *You must be exhausted, dear.*

Now that she mentioned it, I realized I was. It'd been a really long day, what with losing the family sailboat, almost drowning and turning into a mermaid, and swimming off to unknown depths with my boyfriend to meet his family who didn't like me and his old girlfriend who was still so seriously in love with him—yes, I was exhausted.

Why don't you and Shava have a little rest while the rest of us have a family meeting? she said.

I wasn't crazy about being left alone with Shava, but it provided a good opportunity for us to have a little girl-to-girl talk, so I nodded, okay.

I won't be long, Tor added. He seemed to say that to both of us, which just got my blood boiling again.

Tor and his family disappeared deeper into the caves. I folded my arms and stared at Shava. *Look, I know you two had a thing going, but Tor assures me it's over. He and I are together now.*

Instead of protesting, Shava burst into tears. Yes, it turns out you could cry underwater. I would've much preferred protest.

I just love him so much. I've known Tor all my life. We grew up together.

This story sounded oddly familiar, only it was Colby's voice, talking about me. It was weird thinking about Colby while I was who-knew-where under the sea, in a cave think-talking with a sobbing mermaid.

My life had gotten really strange. I focused back on Shava, who was still babbling on.

Then, like all merchildren, when we hit puberty, we were offered the option of going on land. For most of us, the idea of going ashore is very frightening, especially because we're told how painful it is, but Tor has always wanted to do it. He's very brave.

She looked at me with wide mournful eyes and hiccuped and I fought the urge to go hug and comfort her.

Didn't you have the same choice? Why didn't you go?

That comment just triggered more tears.

Shava?

I'm not brave like that. I begged him not to. Kon didn't want him to, either. No one did, but he did it anyway.

It was hard to stay angry with her. I changed the course of the conversation. *Where is everyone else?*

They've gone ahead. We're just waiting for Uncle Dex.

He's your uncle, too?

Through marriage. The queen is my aunt, my mother's sister.

Okay. *Why are you here? Why aren't you with your parents?*

Again she laid her soulful, wide eyes on me. *My mother passed away. My father,* her voice lowered to a whisper, *he was from the other clan.*

Is that bad?

She nodded. *Oh, and I'm so sorry for grabbing your ankle. I only did it because I knew it would bring Tor into the bay.*

She was the one who grabbed my ankle? Not a scuba diver playing a joke. I was too surprised and kind of ticked off to say anything right away.

Now, if you don't mind, I think I'll go to sleep.

I didn't know what I'd expected, for her to go off to some cave bedroom or something, but instead she just closed her eyes. Like a fish in an aquarium, she just hovered in one spot and slept.

It was perturbing.

Hello.

I whipped around, looking for the owner of this new child-like voice. I scanned the cave, but outside of Shava hanging like an oversized piñata, I saw no one.

Down here.

I squinted, but all I could see were short stalks of waving seaweed attached to the cave floor.

Then something rose out of it. I jumped back like I'd spotted a mouse.

Only it was a—seahorse? Atlantic sea horses weren't common and I'd never actually seen one before, but though this creature had a horse shaped head, a skeletal body that floated vertically, and a monkey-like tail wrapped around a thwack of seaweed, it was the size of a man's shoe—too big to be a seahorse.

I'm not a sea horse. I resemble a sea dragon. Obviously, you don't know your sea creatures very well.

Did it really talk to me?

Yes, and my name is Barnaculoese.

I pinched my eyes together. I was just tired, that was all, beyond exhausted.

Are you always so rude, Dori?

It knew my name!

W-what are you?

I'm a sea-nymph.

But sea-nymphs aren't real.

Neither are mermaids.

Touché.

The creature disentangled himself from the seaweed and swam slowly toward me, his body remaining vertical. That was when I saw that many of the seaweed type strands were actually attached to his body, a perfect camouflage, much like the sea dragon. Only sea dragons weren't native to these waters.

He was fascinating in the way reptiles and rodents were to me. Better from a distance, preferably in a cage. I shifted backward slightly.

Okay, Barney, I ventured. *Nice to meet you.*

Likewise. And the name's Barnaculoese.

Right. Fancy name for a fancy fish. *So, what'd you do around here, Barnaculoese? Do the king and queen know about you?*

Of course. I'm their special aide.

As in personal assistant? Their secretary?

His seaweed appendages danced delicately around his body. *Something like that.*

And what is your assignment now?

You are.

I felt a burning flash of anger. I wasn't a prisoner here. And honestly, between Sleeping Shava and Barney the think-talking sea-nymph, I was a little freaked out.

I floated to the entrance.

Dori, you mustn't go out there, Barnaculoese said.

Try and stop me, you little sea horse-monkey. Besides, I could out swim you, you slow-poke-vertical-swimmer, any day.

Apparently Barney disagreed. He flattened out into a horizontal line and zipped passed me like an eel on speed.

I thrust myself out of his way. Did sea-nymphs bite or sting? I really didn't want to find out.

But I also didn't want to be bullied by a pet. Even if it did belong to a king.

Excuse me, Barnaculoese. I feigned self-importance. *But I need to step outside for some, uh, air.*

I swam gingerly toward the mouth of the cave, watching Barney out of the corner of my eye. If he felt the need to shadow me, fine. As long as he kept his slimy little weedy attachments to himself.

I paused briefly when I spotted the guards. If they saw me staring they didn't show any sign. They were big and bulky, almost bigger than Dex. They flanked either side of the cave, staring straight ahead, alert, only their tail fins moving gently to keep them vertical.

I dared to swim out in front, relieved to see Barney had halted behind them.

Hey, I thought-spoke. *How's it going?*

No response. I wondered if I failed to address them properly. I tried again. *Hi, there. I'm Dori. What are your names?*

Nothing. Were they ignoring me? How rude. Or maybe they were like the queen's guards in England, the guys with the big black Q-tips for hats. I swam around and waved my hands.

They didn't budge.

I put my thumbs in my ears and wiggled my fingers. *Na-na-na-na-na-na.*

It was like I was invisible. I laughed.

Then a thunderous sound. *Get back in the cave, Dori Seward of Eastcove. You're too far out.*

Oh. They did speak. Kind of scary, really. I swam back inside like a chastised child.

Barney chuckled.

Oh, shut up.

Shava still hung there, sleeping. I was too attached to my human ways to follow suit. I found a crevice in the wall, a makeshift stone bunk bed and lay down.

I closed my eyes willing myself to relax and trying to push the humiliation I felt with the guard encounter out of my mind, but I couldn't sleep. Barney hovered vertically near my head.

Look, Barnaculoese, I need a bit of space. Can't you watch me from over there? I gestured to the other side of the cave. *I'm obviously not going anywhere.*

Barney dipped his head in a mini bow. *As you wish.*

As you wish? Now he was my genie? I snarfed. I *wished.* No such luck for me.

I took in a big gill breath and tried to settle into the rock "bed." A little sleep would feel really good.

I had to bring her.

My eyes sprung open. That was Tor's voice.

Don't you know she's exactly what they're looking for? Kon? I didn't know why I could hear them all of a sudden. It was like I'd tuned into Tor's radio wave.

She's one of us. She deserved to see our world. Tor.

She's not one of us. And you've brought danger to our clan by bringing her here. Kon.

Father? Tor.

Nothing. As hard as I tried, I couldn't pick up Tor's signal again. One thing was for sure. They were arguing about me.

My chest tightened. I felt claustrophobic. I'd been underwater too long. My lungs weren't use to this and I had an overwhelming need to surface.

I tried to calm myself, focusing on my gills the way Tor had instructed me before, but it didn't work this time. All I could hear was the echo of Kon's voice, "She's not one of us. You've brought danger to our clan by bringing her here."

My heart raced. I feared I would black out. Could a mermaid drown?

Tor? I cried out. *Help?*

Dori? I was shocked at how fast he came to me.

Tor? My lungs. I need to surface.

He took my hand and we swam out of the cave and headed up.

20

It was nighttime. I wasn't sure why this surprised me, since it had been a *long* day. When my head burst through the surface, I drew in a deep breath. It was weird because it wasn't like my body lacked oxygen, but it just felt so good, like a back massage.

Plus, now I could talk with my mouth.

"Tor, that was so intense."

He smiled, but in the moonlight, I saw his eyes. They were heavy.

"What's the matter? What were you and Kon talking about?"

"You could hear us?"

I nodded.

"I guess I was thinking about you too much. You shouldn't have heard that."

"But I did. Why am I a danger?"

Tor let out a long breath. "Can we talk about this tomorrow? We're both tired."

"But *will* we talk about this tomorrow?"

"I promise."

I was so tired I'd probably forget half of what we'd talked about if we did keep going. "Okay. So what now?" We were bobbing on the surface and I wondered if I was just supposed to close my eyes like Shava had.

"Come here." Tor opened his arms and I swam into them, turning to settle my back into his chest as he wrapped his arms around me. "I'll hold you. Go to sleep now."

I melted into his warmth and strength, wishing for every night in my future to end this way. My eyes drooped shut and I drifted off. Time stopped until the sun rose, waking us both with its brightness.

"Good morning, Sunshine." I couldn't tell at first if Tor spoke to me or the actual sun, but the way his eyes sparkled when he looked at me made me believe the former.

"Good morning," I said. I scooped a little seawater for mouthwash. Then I turned in for a kiss. Tor didn't hesitate and kissed me back with warm soft wake-up kisses.

"Hungry?" he said when he pulled away.

"I'm famished." What I wanted more than anything was Mom's fried kipper breakfast with potato pancakes.

Tor pointed to jumping salmon. Okay, raw salmon would do in a pinch. Tor took off and I followed him. The guy could swim really fast when he had a mind to. Then he caught a fish mid air. If I hadn't seen it with my own eyes, I wouldn't have believed it.

"Breakfast!" he shouted proudly. We tore it apart like savages, and I was glad I couldn't watch myself do it. I was sure it wasn't pretty, but boy, was it good. I sucked in the juice of its pink flesh and quenched my growing thirst.

"You're a good fisher merman," I said with a grin.

"Years of practice."

Which took me back to the events of the day before. To Shava's story of how she grew up with Tor, how Tor had always been merfolk, while I was new to the clan, and not welcomed. My heart dropped as I recalled Tor and Kon's conversation.

"Dori?" Tor said.

"I'm remembering yesterday. It didn't go at all like I'd imagined."

"And how was that?"

"Well, I thought your family would be happier to see me," I said, leaving out the part where I didn't exactly expect an old lovelorn girlfriend, either. Or my Disney-esque imagining of what the actual dwelling place would look like. I hadn't expected castles and treasure, but I had expected something... more.

"I'm sorry about that. You were a surprise to them, that's all. Don't take it personally."

"Why am I a danger?"

Tor skimmed around on his back.

"Tor, you promised."

He stopped and faced me. "There is another clan..."

"You mentioned that."

"Many generations back, there was only one clan. Legend has it that two brothers, Lars and Rai, were promised the blessing of their father, but only one could reign royally over the sea.

"The older brother, Lars, thought he had the crown for sure due to his birthright. Except that he and his mate didn't conceive. When his younger brother, Rai, had an heir, Lars was consumed with jealousy. Rai would now inherit the crown, and the royal title.

"So Lars took Rai's wife against her will and they

conceived. Rai, of course, was enraged, and took his complaint to their father, who sided with the younger son.

"The father accused Lars of impatience and imprudence. If only he had waited and stayed true to his mate he would've eventually conceived an heir and would have had rightful title to the throne.

"But, because Lars had disgraced his family with his actions, he and his mate were banned from the family.

"Lars did eventually conceive with his mate, but it was too late for the blessing of his father."

"Lars is the other clan," I said.

Tor nodded. "Part of the blessing that Lars missed out on is the ability and the choice to go ashore. To live with the humans."

Tor looked to the sky, measuring how far the sun had risen. "We should go back now. We've been away too long."

I was about to protest. I still didn't have all the answers I wanted, but Tor had already disappeared under the water.

I followed him, watching his tattoos swirling on his broad shoulders as he swam gracefully through the currents, certain where he was going.

I, on the other hand, still had no idea, and would be horribly lost if I had to find my own way back to Eastcove. Obviously, my instinct skills were underdeveloped as well.

A reddish-green swoosh of motion startled me. Something encircled us. Something fast.

Tor pulled me close, shielding me with his body. Fear rocked my heartbeat.

I heard Tor's voice. *Reveal yourself!*

The blur slowed and an image formed.

A merman? He was smaller than Tor or any member of Tor's family. His tail had more red than green and though he looked muscular, his skin was smooth and glossy like a jelly fish, not like the human skin that Tor's clan had. His tattoos had the same rosy sheen as his tail. He must be a member to the clan of Lars.

When he spoke, I could hear him. *Prince Mol wants her.*

Too bad. Tor scoffed.

Why would he want *me?* This little merman was antsy, swishing around us. I scanned the area looking for others. The way Tor's head swiveled, I could tell he was doing the same.

Are there more? I said, trying really hard to focus my thoughts on Tor. I didn't want the creature to hear my fear.

I don't think so. If there were other spies, they would've showed themselves by now.

I stumbled on the word, "spies" but another part of my brain understood that if there were others from the Lars clan, Tor would be injured by now, or worse, and I would be captured.

I wondered how gross it would be to throw up underwater?

Shall we fight it out, Cho?

Cho, the spy, didn't jump on Tor's offer. I was encouraged by this. His homely little face twisted in thought.

You're alone, aren't you? Tor continued. *They sent you out by yourself again. Do you ever wonder why? I believe it's because they don't think you'll ever find anything of interest and this is how they get you out of their hair.*

Cho's face scrunched up until he looked like a blowfish, turning as red as his tail.

Shut up! I see her, she's real and Prince Mol will want her and he will have her, one way or another.

He might be a small upstart of a spy, but he freaked me out.

Why should they believe you? You've never produced anything of value before, and you have no proof.

Tor shouldn't have said that.

In a flash, the water swooshed and I felt a pinch in my head.

Ouch.

Cho! Tor shouted, but the weasel was gone. And he had a chunk of my hair as proof.

21

How did he find me?

Tor led me back to the cave, and hopefully out of harm's way. *He could smell you.*

He could smell me? I serendipitously sniffed my armpit. *If Cho could smell me, why didn't he find us at the surface last night?*

The clan of Lars doesn't surface, Tor said. *They don't have lungs, at least not lungs developed enough to breathe air. Plus, they have more predators than we do.*

Why's that? The curse?

Tor's head bobbed. *Because of that, they're shy of open water, but that doesn't mean they wouldn't go there if they wanted something bad enough. They'd just do it with larger numbers.*

How many of them are there? Are the clans the same size?

Ironically, the clan of Lars did grow more rapidly than the clan of Rai. That was the one blessing that remained.

More Lars than Rai. I wasn't happy to hear that.

Are they all as homely as that?

No.

I puzzled over that answer. Was there a pretty mermaid in that clan, too? Maybe Shava wasn't my only competition. But I wasn't in Eastcove anymore where I could obsess over petty things like that. I had real problems now. Life and death problems.

Why is he so interested in me? And who is this Prince Mol?

Tor stiffened. *It's complicated.*

I think I can get it.

All right. You deserve to know, but let's get back to the cave first, where you'll be safe.

Kon was waiting outside the cave when we arrived, his face stern.

What is it, Kon? Tor said.

Kon's eyes flitted quickly toward me, his brow wrinkling in a scowl. He so obviously didn't like me. I wondered how two brothers could be so different. The bigger, older brother hadn't gone ashore when he'd had the chance, the younger brother had—despite Kon's objections, if Shava could be trusted as a reliable source of information.

He focused back on Tor, but I could still hear him.

It was here. A spy.

Tor moved protectively in front of me. *We know. We ran into Cho on the way here. One of them is nothing.*

Kon folded his arms over his—I'd have to admit—impressive chest, and huffed. *One for now. More later, and who knows how many more. Tor, she's not worth it. You have to take her back.*

I wasn't worth it?

If you don't, I will.

Watch it brother, Tor said, matching Kon's tone.

Kon swam up to Tor, until he was only an arm's length away, his hands curling into fists at his side. Tor's shoulders rolled back, his chest puffed out.

Were they really going to fight each other because of me?

Wait, wait, wait! I shouted.

They pulled back.

Don't I have something to say about this?

This isn't your business, Kon spit out.

How is it not my business? You're talking about me.

Only in how your presence presents a danger to our clan.

Oh. Not my clan. I didn't have a clan. What did that make me? A merfolk type of lone ranger. An anomaly?

I waited for Tor to come to my defense. I shot him a pleading look and when he didn't speak up, my heart sank.

Let's take this inside the cave, Tor, Kon said. *I have a feeling the king and queen will side with me.*

He swam away quickly. I felt sick. Would Tor really send me home? I literally felt myself sinking.

Tor dove to grab my arm and pulled me up. He pointed over my shoulder.

Look who's here?

Dex! I was so happy to see a familiar and friendly face that I swam to him, and made a fool of myself by wrapping my arms around his thick neck.

He laughed. *Hello, Dori.* He put his log-sized arm around me in response and squeezed. This act of kindness almost brought me to tears. I wasn't used to being the outsider. Back in Eastcove, people liked me. They thought I was talented and intelligent, cute and fun to hang around.

It's so good to see you, Uncle Dex. I didn't know why I used the familiar term, "uncle." We were in no way related, but besides Tor, he seemed like my only ally here. So much had happened in the last few days that Dex had gone from being Tor's aloof uncle, to my personal friend who understood me! I never said I was being rational.

Dex's white hair and beard floated around him, much like

my hair did. I took a moment to absorb his new look. Bare shoulders with strength that could lift a boulder were covered with intricate tattoos complex in pattern and color. I'd never seen him without a shirt on before, and I was taken aback by his beauty. His massive deep royal-blue tail swished gently, keeping him upright.

He suddenly seemed so regal that I had to fight the urge to bow in deference.

You look different, too, he said with a smile. Then added kindly, *We should go inside.*

We swam past the royal guards, who never moved out of position but acknowledged Dex with a bow. I wondered where they got their weapons from, but of course, Dex and Tor could've provided them.

Again, I was blind inside the cave but this time it didn't take as long for my eyes to adjust. The king and queen and Shava were there. Kon took his position on the right side of the king.

Dex, King Playo said. He bowed slightly then moved in to shake Dex's hand. I found it odd that the king would bow to anyone, but then I knew next to nothing about merfolk customs.

The queen, Kon and Shava, all bowed when they greeted Dex. Must be a custom reserved for elders. I'd have to remember to bow to Dex next time, instead of mauling him like a crazed fan.

There is activity stirring up from all sides, King Playo said.

Kon added, *Spies have entered our territory.* He looked accusingly at me. *They can smell her.*

I hated how he made it sound like I stank. I didn't, did I?

We've got pods of Rai situated strategically, Dex said. *We're in a good defensive position.*

Still, we haven't much time, Kon insisted. *We shouldn't*

wait for them to come to us, and now we have something they want.

A little fear-filled shiver slithered down my spine. I was what they wanted, but I still didn't know why.

We need to leave as soon as possible, the King said. *It would be best if she weren't here as an excuse for them to attack.*

Yes, brother, you are right. Dex turned to Tor. *You have to take her back. We knew that this could happen when we agreed to let her come.*

I wanted to jump up and down and stomp my feet. *Stop talking about me like I'm not here!*

All the eyes in the room widened. I didn't think they all realized I could hear them.

Why am I such a danger? I demanded. *Why do they want me?*

Silence. No one wanted to tell me. Why? Was it really that horrible?

I've told her about the legend, Tor said, finally.

So, then you know about the two clans, Uncle Dex said, *and the blessing that the clan of Lars missed out on?*

I nodded. Little nervous twitches shot through my tail. I wanted to know and I was afraid to know. I waited for someone to tell me. Tor? The king or queen? Or Barney, who appeared suddenly out of the darkness and hovered by the queen's shoulder?

It was Dex who spoke.

More than anything the clan of Lars wants to be able to go ashore, to be able to dwell among the humans. They hate us because we can and they can't. Our ability to go on land gives us many advantages, primarily with information and technology. The clan of Rai is like the early land tribe who had fire; it gave them potential and power. All the other tribes would war with that one tribe just to get the fire.

Okay. So, what does that have to do with me?

Dex shifted his arms uncomfortably. Now I was really nervous.

The only way the tribe of Lars can ever hope to be land dwellers is for their prince to mate with someone who is human. Of course, since they can't go on land, this can never happen with someone who is fully human. They need a girl who is part human and part merfolk, so that their offspring can share her traits.

Someone like me?

Yes, Uncle Dex said. I looked at Tor; he found it hard to keep my gaze. This kind of talk was uncomfortable for them.

And they will fight you to get me, I said, the truth working like a vice grip around my heart. I felt faint.

Kon was right. I had to go. It was the right thing to do, not only for the sake of the clan of Rai, but also, I was finally admitting, for my family in Eastcove.

My heart was crushed. Going home meant being away from Tor, for who knew how long.

I didn't have a chance to worry about this. A deep voice bellowed from the cave entrance.

On guard!

Kon and Dex quickly moved in front of the king and queen. Kon pulled Shava in behind him. Tor moved in front of me.

What's going on? I said to Tor

Cho's returned and he's not alone.

22

*D*ex swam toward the guards. *Keep them back,* he instructed Kon. Then to Tor. *Don't let go of her.*

I could see through a sliver opening between Dex and the guards. A handful, maybe five or six Larsfolk, treading water like egg beaters. They were the ADHD version of Tor's clan.

I was freaking out because I knew they wanted me, and now I knew *why.*

There's only five, Tor said to Kon. *Why?*

They must have had a small pod stationed nearby. They've come to see if the spy's news was true or not.

What will they do? I moaned. *Will they fight?*

Not this time, their numbers are too low, Tor said. *Besides, they must know the king and queen of Rai are here.*

Dex's voice boomed. *What is your business here?*

A high-pitched whiny voice responded. *We want to see the girl.*

What girl?

We know there is a girl, neither Lars nor Rai. Our spy provided a strand of hair as proof.

I turned to Tor. *How could they tell by a strand of my hair? I imagined them examining it through an underwater microscope.*

They could smell it.

Smells again? I was going to get a complex.

What did they smell?

Human.

Oh. I didn't smell like merfolk. I smelled human. I really didn't belong here.

If there is a girl such as you claim in our midst, Dex said, I have no intention of presenting her to you. Therefore, I urge you to leave.

We will not leave until we see her.

Are you declaring war? You are aware that the king and queen of Rai are with us?

This information seemed to shake them. I shot Tor a questioning look.

It is against merfolk rules of war to engage battle directly with royalty, unless their own king or prince declare war first.

Tor turned to Kon. *Is there another way out?*

Kon nodded then questioned his parents.

Should I take them?

I believe we are fine for the moment, King Playo said. You and Tor remove the girl. Dex and the guards are handling the matter.

Tor squeezed my hand.

The king continued, *You should move on. We'll find you at the next stop.*

Oh, Tor! The queen reached out for her son, her eyes full of motherly concern. *It's not safe for you to travel alone right now.*

There's no other way. I'll be careful Mother, I promise. Tor kissed her quickly on the cheek.

Then he turned to Shava. Her eyes were wide with fear

and, I would dare to say, longing. The look she shared with Tor was like a punch in the gut to me. There was nothing that would keep Shava from pursuing Tor when he returned without me. I was sure of this.

All the stress was causing my lungs to seize up again.

This way, Kon said. He swam further into the back regions of the cave. I held tightly to Tor's hand, praying my eyes would continue to adapt to the growing blackness. I hoped the way out wouldn't take long. The walls of the cave felt like they were pressing in, and I fought the growing panic of being trapped in dark, closed in spaces.

Tor! I can't do this. It's too deep, too dark. My pulse. I can't breathe.

Hold up, Kon. Tor stopped and wrapped his arms around me. *Close your eyes, Dori. Count to ten.* I breathed in and out, my eyes pinched close.

Imagine we're sitting on our rock in Eastcove.

He called it *our* rock. It was our rock! I felt myself calm as I pictured us sitting there, the wind blowing in our hair. Sidney barking. I let the peace of that image settle over me.

I focused on my gills filling my being with oxygen until I felt light.

I think I'm okay now, I said.

Good. Tor took my hand and we followed Kon deeper into the cave tunnel.

There was a system of caves strung together like beads of various sizes. Large cavernous spaces connected to much smaller caves with only room for two. Each was attached by a narrow passage we had to swim through horizontally and in single file.

Okay, I was panicking. It didn't matter how much I thought about our rock or the fact that my gills did an adequate job of supplying my oxygen requirements, I hated, hated, hated being in tight, dark enclosed places. I hadn't known that about myself, but I'd never squished myself into a barrel and had someone throw me into the ocean before, either.

My mouth was wide open and I knew I was screaming. I squeezed Tor's hand so tightly, I was sure I must've been cutting off his circulation.

He sensed my distress. *Dori? Are you okay?*

No, I'm freaking not okay. Get me out of here! As an afterthought I added, *Please.*

How much farther? Tor said.

We're almost there, Kon answered.

Almost there, almost there.

I squeezed my eyes shut and forced myself to picture East-cove, the beauty of the boats at the pier, the summer energy of the boardwalk. My mind flashed to Becca and Samara doing normal things like lying in the sun and reading magazines. I thought of the endless cycle of school and ordinary school days where nothing was ever new, especially some hot guy. I focused on all the summers before this one that were totally uneventful and boring.

Anything but what I was experiencing now.

I remembered swimming in a nice symmetrical rectangle pool, totally safe, when my only enemy was my swim competition. And sometimes Colby. I thought of his buzz cut and how soothing it was to rub his head.

Tor jerked my arm slightly.

Oh, man, could he tell I was thinking about Colby?

I was overwhelmed by a hollow sense of defeat. My romantic dream of joining my underworld family and swimming away into the sunset with the love of my life was a complete and miserable FAIL.

Honestly, what else could go wrong?

Finally, the darkness brightened slightly. Kon pointed at

the exit and came to a full stop. *I'll see you at the next meeting point, brother.* The earlier animosity he displayed was absent now that he was getting his way.

Thanks for bringing us this far, Tor said.

Kon nodded goodbye to me and turned back into the blackness of the cave tunnels. That was all the farewell I deserved, seeing the trouble I'd caused in such a short time.

We swam away, and I was relieved to see open water. My lungs were really screaming now.

Tor, I need to surface. Please.

When we broke the surface, I sucked in a deep, ragged breath.

"Just make sure you don't break the water with your tail," Tor said. Not, are you okay? Or, come here, let me hold you, not anything reassuring.

The wind had picked up and the surface was choppy, splashing waves over my head.

Tor scanned the horizon over my shoulder. "A storm's brewing."

Great. More problems.

"We have to keep moving, but we can stay near the surface until you feel up to submerging again."

The wind whipped up overhead, the waves capping with frothy white tips. Tor's expression remained stern.

"Let's keep going." He was all business now, and I was certain that I had dropped down the ladder of importance for Tor. The question was, how far?

We swam in silence for so long, I'd lost track of time. Maybe it was the gray sky blending with the water, or the noise of the wind overtaking any other sound, or maybe we were just too focused on our destination.

I didn't see Crazy Jim's fishing boat until it was too late. And I made the worst possible mistake.

I broke the water with my tail.

Of course Crazy Jim would see that. Not my sailboat yesterday in calm water or me screaming for help, but my tail in stormy weather.

Then I heard a gunshot.

Tor heard it too. He grabbed my hand and pulled me under. Crazy Jim didn't mean he would catch a *live* mermaid to prove his claims. He meant dead or alive.

Tor pulled me deeper and I breathed hyperactively through my gills, my lungs felt like they'd flattened my chest like heated lead. *Tor! I need to go back up!*

We can't. He's shooting at us. Tor placed his hands on both sides of my face. *Look me in the eyes, Dori. You're breathing. You have gills, just focus on them.*

I tried to focus but all I could think about was how stupid I was to think, that after having a tail for less than an hour, I could seamlessly integrate with merfolk and life under the sea.

Dori, we have to keep going.

I nodded weakly and let Tor guide me.

I wasn't sure how fast Tor could swim, but even as a mermaid, I couldn't out swim a boat going full throttle. My only hope was that the rough weather would continue to be our ally, and force Crazy Jim to slow down.

Then the unbelievable happened.

Tor! I shouted. Out of the corner of my eye, I saw a body drop past us. Tor stopped and watched as Crazy Jim sank, his arms flailing, weighed down by all his clothing and heavy boots. He must've slid off the slippery deck when his boat lurched.

Tor swam rapidly, scooped him up under his arms and headed up to the surface. He was saving Crazy Jim's life? After he'd just tried to kill us?

I had no choice but to follow, since I couldn't take the chance of getting separated from Tor.

Tor broke the surface with Crazy Jim in his arms. Crazy Jim coughed and gurgled as Tor wrestled to put him on the lower ledge at the boat's stern.

I gulped air with my lungs, just glad to surface again. We waited until Crazy Jim got his footing and climbed back into his boat.

His expression was wild and crazed, like he couldn't believe he'd just been rescued by a merman. I could only imagine the stories he would tell now when he got back to East-cove. My heart collapsed. Now that Crazy Jim had spotted more merfolk, and in fact had made contact with one, he would never let this story die. Tor and Dex were never coming back.

We'd waited too long.

Crazy Jim wasn't about to let his proof get away. He raised his gun again.

Searing pain ripped through my tail. A stream of red floated around me—a crimson ribbon.

I'd been shot by Crazy Jim. I felt myself slipping, and then I was gone.

23

—————

I was screaming when I came to.

I was also dry. Lying on something hard. Breathing with my lungs.

It was all coming into focus, slowly like an old Polaroid picture.

I cried out again.

"Dori." Tor's face flashed in front of mine. "You're going to be okay, it's almost over."

The pain struck my legs again; my left leg was in particular misery.

I held on to Tor, breathing through the pain. Then I did something I hadn't done in over twenty-four hours. I wiggled my toes.

"Where are we?" I croaked.

"On the rock by the cave."

I dared to look around. The sky was still dark with the impending storm, the wind whipping my hair across my face. Tor sat beside me wearing the clothes he had on yesterday, the ones he'd tucked away in the rocks before we left.

I gasped with the sudden knowledge that I was lying on the rock, nude. I glanced down at my lower body and breathed. Tor had draped the sweatpants I'd discarded over my nakedness.

My left leg stuck out, with a piece of cloth tied above an angry red wound. That was when I saw the t-shirt I was wearing was torn.

Tor saw me analyzing it. "I had to tear a strip off your shirt to cut off the flow of blood."

"How come you're already dressed?"

"I transformed more quickly than you." He frowned. "Maybe because I'm not injured."

I tried to move my leg and groaned. "How bad?"

"It's only a flesh wound," Tor said. "No severed arteries or shredded muscle groups." Tor ripped a section from the T-shirt he had on and gently applied it like a bandage. I tried not to moan too loudly.

"Dori, it's going to pour rain soon. We should go in."

I sat up, blocking out the pain, and wondered how I was going to get into the sweat pants. I wished I wasn't so modest. Tor was every bit the gentleman and, it turned out, a capable nurse.

"I'll help you, and I promise I won't look."

I almost laughed at that. He was true to his word, and then he gently carried me up the rocks to his former home.

I thought the cave would be empty, but Uncle Dex had left just enough stuff, like he thought one of them might return. I supposed he totally expected Tor to return with me. He had been right. One day.

A cot, a blanket, a box of crackers and a bottle of water. If anyone did happen to come upon this cave accidentally, and I couldn't imagine it, it would just look like campers abandoning some of their stuff. Same with the clothing we left behind on the rocks.

Still it was dry, and Tor drew me in close to him as we lay together on the cot. His body heat kept me warm.

"I'm sorry you were injured." He couldn't look me in the eye when he said this, and I knew he felt remorseful.

"It's okay."

He looked hard at me, then. "No, it's not. You could've been killed."

"But I wasn't." I pulled him closer, hoping to comfort him.

I had to ask. "Tor, why'd you do it?"

"Do what?"

"Rescue Crazy Jim. You do realize he was trying to kill us?"

"We're taught in the clan of Rai from a very young age to do the right thing, even if others around us are doing the wrong thing."

"Like the clan of Lars?"

"Yeah, but not just them. Also humans."

That answer surprised me. "What do you mean?"

"Humankind is responsible for many ecological hazards and disasters. Our transient nature in many ways is due to the fact that humans are ruining our home."

I remembered the list of shame. "Over fishing, pollution, oil spills?"

"To name a few. Hypothetically, the clan of Rai could use its powers to live on land as a means to extract revenge, but because of our principles and beliefs, we don't."

I'd never thought of that.

"It's the main reason why it's imperative that the clan of Lars never finds a way on shore."

"They wouldn't do the right thing?"

"Some might, but most wouldn't, especially not Prince Mol."

The state of actual danger I was in under the ocean was growing clearer.

"Why did you let me go with you, then? Despite my extreme obstinacy?"

"I guess I didn't think the danger would be so imminent. And I was selfish. I wanted you with me."

His words flooded me with warm fuzzy feelings, and I snuggled in closer. I loved the feel of his arms wrapped around me. And I loved him. I did. I was sorry he couldn't read my mind now, because, I was too afraid to say it aloud.

I turned my face up and he stared steadily into my eyes. His filled with emotion, and I thought maybe he loved me, too. He leaned down and I was sure of it. His kisses were urgent and passionate. I melted into him, wishing that this moment would never end.

We listened to the wind whistling through the cracks, and watched as the darkened sky flashed with lightening. I clung to Tor, thankful for the shelter of the cave.

Eventually the storm passed. Fingers of sunlight streamed through the thinning clouds, until Eastcove was once again brightened by sunshine.

"We have to get you home," Tor said with a sigh. "You need to see a doctor."

My leg hurt like mad, and I couldn't rest my full weight on it.

Tor helped me up, and put his arm under my left shoulder. I hopped out of the cave, cupping my eyes against the sunlight. Tor managed to lift me up and over the rocks, bit by bit, and I was once again amazed by his strength and agility.

"I don't want to go down the boardwalk, or Main Street," I said.

Tor was in agreement, and we took a back route, even though it was longer. It would be better not to be spotted like this. Plus, I wanted to drag the time Tor and I had together out for as long as possible.

Every hop was painful, but it was balanced out by the comfort I had holding Tor close to me.

When we reached our yard, I almost cried. Not because I was home, though I was really glad to be there. But because Tor was going to say good-bye, and I didn't know when I'd see him again.

We stopped before anyone could spot us, hidden by the thick foliage that surrounded my house.

"Dori?" Tor's voice caught and it scared me.

"Yes?"

"I'm saying good-bye now."

"I know. How long until you come back?"

Tor let his head drop. "That's the thing. I'm not coming back."

My vision blurred, blackness forming at the corners of my eyes.

"Dori?" Tor caught me. I felt him guide me to a garden chair in our back yard.

"Why?" I whimpered.

"I shouldn't have let myself get attached to you in the first place. But, at the time I thought there was a chance I could really make my home here, and when you showed signs of having merfolk traits, I let myself hope. After I researched your ancestry and discovered the possibility that you could be one of us, well, I was really, really happy about that.

"I didn't anticipate that I would be taking you to meet my clan so soon, and in inopportune circumstances. But...I see now, it was a big mistake, and I'm so sorry for dragging you into this."

"Tor, no, it wasn't a mistake. It's just a setback."

"No, Dori. I have to go and you can't come with me. Ever. It's too dangerous. I could never live with myself if something happened to you. And Prince Mol would never give up trying to get you."

Tor's eyes glossed over with sadness. "I'm sorry, Dori. I can't be with someone I can't stay with."

Like Shava. I remembered him saying the same thing about her.

We were startled by the creaking of the screen door.

"It's your mother," Tor whispered. He kissed me, softly, a little groan escaping before he disappeared into the bush. I knew he was running toward the ocean.

It all happened so fast. I didn't have a chance to say what I really wanted to say. That I was in love with Tor Riley.

My heart shattered into a zillion little pieces.

24

I leaned with a crutch against Tor's rock. Our rock. I ended up getting nine stitches, but the prognosis was for a full recovery—physical, anyway.

Everything here looked exactly the same as before—the rocky beach, circling seagulls, sailboats dotting the horizon.

Sidney sat at my feet, panting contently.

I stared out at the ocean, searching for Tor. I knew it was crazy. He was gone, who knew where, and a part of me hoped that he was as crushed as I was.

I recalled the last kiss we shared in his cave, the one where I thought he was telling me he loved me. I knew now he was actually just saying goodbye.

He'd already decided by then.

I was so angry with him I wanted to spit. I forgot momentarily about my injury and kicked at the pebbles with my good leg. My wounded leg couldn't hold my weight and I fell hard to the ground. I thrashed my body like a two-year-old having a tantrum, allowing gigantic tears to run amuck on my face.

The dampness of the sand seeped through my clothes. I

reluctantly picked myself up and stumbled around awkwardly with my crutch, trying to get a grip in the moving sand. As much as I'd love to just let the tide sweep me out to the sea, I knew I couldn't stay here forever.

"Come on, Sidney." I propped myself up on the crutch and hobbled down the path. It was a cumbersome venture, and I had to be careful not to trip on twigs or root systems pushing through the earth.

There was a strange dirt bike—new— in the yard when I got home. The owner turned to face me.

Colby.

"Hey, Seaweed."

We hadn't seen each other since I'd been back and hadn't spoken since that time on the dock when I'd shoved the letter declaring I was clean in his face.

He offered a cautious smile—a peace offering. I offered one back.

Then he stroked the side of the brand new glossy red bike. "What'd'ya think?"

"Is it yours?"

"Yup. My parents paid for half. Birthday present."

Sometime between my becoming a mermaid and my nine stitches, Colby had had a birthday. I should've remembered. It was three days before mine.

"Happy Birthday," I said.

"Happy Birthday to you, too."

Today I was sixteen. I didn't want to celebrate and no one dared to make me.

"I would rather have gotten a car," Colby said, "but hey." He produced a second helmet. A hopeful grin on his face. "Do you want to go for a ride?"

"I'm kind of injured here."

"I'll go easy."

I wondered where Tiffany was, and why she wasn't getting this offer. Then I realized I didn't care.

"Consider it my birthday gift to you."

"Okay."

Colby helped me keep my balance as I lifted my gimpy leg over the bike seat. His grip on my waist felt good, almost like a hug.

His dark eyes held mine and I lifted my hand. He grinned, knowing what I wanted and leaned down so I could reach. His brush cut was soft and comforting and it shook off the residue of my recent tantrum.

He handed me my helmet, then slipped into place in front of me. I wrapped my arms tightly around him and pressed my face into his back. I could feel his chest expand as he breathed.

He pushed down on the kick-start and revved the engine. The jerk and vibration rattled my leg, and I winced with the pain.

Colby turned to me. "You okay?"

I nodded. "Yes."

"So, Seaweed, where do you wanna go?"

I didn't have to think long. "Anywhere."

I welcomed the pain that shot up my leg as we rode along the trail—it helped to block out the searing ache that squeezed my heart. The wind whipped at my eyes forcing them shut, which I hated because Tor's face kept taunting my mind.

The engine slowed and Colby brought the bike to a stop. We were at the crest of a cliff overlooking the ocean. I inhaled the salty air and scanned the horizon.

The ocean's roar called to me and it hit me then—I could never go in it again. In fact, unless I wanted to become a mermaid, *all* swimming was out of the question. Swimming was my life before Tor Riley. My hopes for a scholarship and a way out of Eastcove were gone with him. This was what he'd stolen from me.

The high wire of grief I'd been balancing on tightened. It thickened into something else. Anger? Betrayal?

"Hey." Colby pointed.

We saw it at the same time, just before the head bobbed under the surface. My heart stuttered.

"A seal?" he said.

"Yeah," I whispered.

A seal with deep-set green eyes.

25

My parents wanted answers. There were three main things that didn't line up: The boat wreck, my lie about going to Becca's and my gunshot wound. Crafting a story that explained these things, plus the fact that I'd been missing for a day and a half took a skill I didn't possess.

All I could do was apologize. I did tell them I'd been hit and shot by Crazy Jim, which correlated with the tales he was telling everyone who'd listen.

"He thought you were a *mermaid*?" Mom had asked.

But when it came to where I was and why I'd lied, I obviously couldn't answer them. This didn't go over well, let's just say.

I would've been grounded if it weren't for the fact that I'd nearly been killed. I guessed they figured my nine stitches and broken heart were enough punishment.

Yeah, I also had to try to explain Tor's sudden departure. My parents weren't stupid; they knew I wasn't giving them the whole story.

Samara and Becca were ticked off, too. They couldn't

understand why I wouldn't tell them what had happened. We'd never kept secrets from each other before and I'd thrown up some kind of barrier by being the first to conceal. They tried to act like it didn't bother them, but I knew them too well. After a couple attempts at forced amusement over magazines and fake laughter at bad jokes, I'd started to decline their invites to get together. Before too long, they'd stopped making them.

The day of my tantrum, aka my birthday, was also the last time I'd been to the beach near our house. Actually, it was the last time I'd gone to any beach. I just couldn't bear to be near the ocean. It only reminded me of all that I'd lost.

Instead I started taking Sidney for a walk to the park on the other side of Nana's house. It had a playground and a big lawn and was safely tucked into the edge of the forest. Not that I wanted to talk to Nana; I'd skip around the back so I wouldn't accidentally bump into her. I wasn't ready to ask her the many questions I had. I was too afraid of the answers.

Every evening after dinner I'd escape with Sidney to get away from the effort my family made to bring me back from the emotional dead. And every evening Colby would drive by on his dirt bike and pick me up.

Dear, stable, never changing, reliable, adorable Colby. The boy I wished I could love.

It was the end of summer, the last weekend before school. I was half way to the park when I heard the rev of Colby's bike.

He slowed when he reached me.

"Hey."

"Hey." I accepted the extra helmet he always carried for me. I suppressed my urge to wince as I threw my injured leg over. The stitches were out, but the scar would always be there. A permanent reminder of the suckiest summer ever.

Colby kicked it into gear, but kept the speed down so Sidney could keep up.

At the park we'd lay on our backs on the grass and stare at the stars.

"Can't believe school starts in three days," Colby said. "Only two more years of high school."

I grunted. Only two more years until Colby went to some hot university on a swim scholarship and I headed off to a local college so I could stay home and work my way through school.

Colby rolled over onto his side. I did the same and faced him.

"Dori, everything will be better again, once school starts. Things will be the way they were... before."

My mouth pinched. Things could never go back to the way they were before.

"When are you gonna come back to swim club? You'd feel so much better if you'd just come back."

I pulled myself up to sitting position and hugged my knees. "I can't go back, Colby."

He sat up to face me. "Look, I said I was sorry. How many times do I have to apologize?"

"That's not why I'm not coming back."

"Then why?"

I stared up at the stars, wishing I could tell him. Wishing I could tell someone. Instead I just shrugged.

Colby let it go. "Do you remember when we were in first grade and we were invited to Sawyer's birthday party?"

I felt a smile pull at my lips. "Our mothers' dressed us to the nines for some reason."

"You wore a pink princess dress with a load of frills."

I blushed that he'd remembered what I was wearing.

"Instead of playing pin the tail on the donkey with the other kids, we snuck off to swim in Sawyer's little sister's kiddy pool. In our dress clothes."

I actually laughed a little at the memory. "Splashing around with you was a blast, but Mom was furious that I'd ruined that dress. It was cheap, all the dye seeped out."

"That's right. The pool water turned pink. And instead of crying about your dress you laughed hilariously. That was the moment I knew."

My gazed jumped to his. "Knew what?"

"That I was crazy about you."

He'd liked me since Sawyer's sixth birthday party?

I couldn't pull my eyes away from his. The pain we shared crackled between us. I reached for his head, an impulse to diffuse the hurt somehow, as if I could magically absorb his, and he could absorb mine. The soft bristles of his brush cut in my palm calmed me. Colby's eyes were soft and warm like pools of hot fudge sundae. He leaned in.

I knew what he wanted. A kiss.

A kiss would change everything, catapult us into a whole other fragile universe. His lips were full and inviting.

But they weren't Tor's lips, and he was the one I still longed for.

I whispered, "I'm not ready."

Colby exhaled. "Okay. I can wait."

His hand brushed lightly against mine. "Can I at least hold your hand?"

Why not? I nodded.

He threaded his fingers through mine. His hand felt different than Tor's. Broader, rougher.

We lay back down on our backs, hands locked between our bodies. The moon rose to spy on us. Did it see the little tear that slid down the side of my face?

26

"*D*ori!" Mom called up the steps. "The rest of us are already at the table."

I sighed and dragged myself off the bed. It was our weekly Sunday brunch and I could smell a waft of fried bacon floating up the stairs. I slipped on my purple fuzzy slippers and headed down.

I heard my mother's voice. "This can't go on forever."

"It's her first crush. She'll get over it eventually." Dad.

"This is exactly why I discourage high school romance." Mom again. "They should just focus on school at this age. They have their whole lives ahead of them for heartache."

Luke: "I'm sick of all the moping. It's like a black cloud has blown through the house."

Dad: "She'll get over it eventually."

"Has she told anyone what happened, yet?" Nana. Freak. I was so not ready to deal with her.

"We know what happened," Mom said tersely. "She got hit by a boat, shot at and almost drowned."

"But she was missing," Nana pressed

"She still won't talk about it," Mom answered. "Believe me, I've tried to get her to talk."

The bottom step squeaked. Mom hushed everyone as I entered. I pretended I hadn't heard them talking about me and took my seat.

Dad chirped, "Mark called. He's settling in at the campus in Calgary."

"Yes," Mom added, too enthusiastically. "He's excited about his first year there."

Warning: Awkward, forced conversation ahead.

"Pass the syrup." I waved in the general direction of the bottle of maple syrup. Luke handed it to me, and I poured it on my stack of pancakes. Nana sat across from me, but I kept my eyes down.

"Are you guys ready for school tomorrow?" Mom asked.

Luke nodded. "Ready enough."

Pause.

Oh, I was supposed to talk. "Uh yeah, me, too."

More pausing.

Mom threw her napkin on the table. "This is crazy. Dori, why don't you just go back to swim club. You need to get back to your old self again."

"Mom, swim club is the last thing I need."

"Why? You love swimming. And you're good at it. It'll take your mind off ... things."

Nana surprised me by answering. "Just because the girl is good at something, doesn't mean she has to do it forever. Dori might want to try other things. I'm sure she could be just as good at something new."

She caught my eye and I read her deeper meaning. I should find an alternate passion if I knew what was good for me. Something that would take me as far away from the ocean as possible.

"Yeah, I'm thinking about basket weaving." I stood. "Thanks for breakfast, Mom. It was delicious."

I left the table so that they could continue to discuss what was best for me in peace.

A new message waited for me in my inbox. Samara and Becca were discussing what they're going to wear on the first day of school.

It was our annual tradition. I followed the thread like a lurker as they discussed which shirt and what shoes.

I'd become a lurker.

Then suddenly, **Are you there, Dori?**

The moment of truth. Did I reply all, or pretend I wasn't here.

Something twigged me. I missed them. I quickly typed, Yes, and sent it before I lost my nerve.

I didn't know I'd been holding my breath. I let it out slowly as I joined in the conversation. I was going to wear jeans and a green shirt. My sneakers. Boring, I know. I typed out my decision and pressed send.

The next morning the alarm misfired. Or maybe I just slammed the snooze button too hard, but I woke up late. I hurried into the promised jeans, shirt and sneakers. I made sure my back-to-school shirts all had sleeves now since I had these tattoos covering my shoulders. So far I'd managed to keep them hidden and I thought I'd be good at least until next summer, when I'd have to come up with another good story.

I paused long enough to run a brush through my hair and sponge washed my face. Another thing I gave up for Tor. Hot baths and showers. Thankfully mere dampness wasn't enough to set off the scales and tail.

No time for make-up, but oddly, I didn't care. Even though it was the first day of school.

"Mom, I'm sorry. I slept in," I said as I grabbed a piece of toast. "Can you walk, Sidney this morning?"

Mom tilted her head like she was annoyed.

"Just a short walk. I'll walk him again after school, I promise."

Mom poured me a glass of juice. "Okay, but just this once, Dori. He's your dog. That was the deal."

I uttered, "Thanks" then rushed to brush my teeth. Luke waited for me in the Rotten Apple.

"Get in. I don't want to be late, first day."

I saw Samara and Becca near the front door of the school, each wearing their preplanned wardrobe choices and huddling together with another girl I couldn't see. I approached them from behind and heard Samara's voice. "She's not been the same since him."

"I don't know what the big deal is. You'd think she was the only girl on the planet who'd ever been dumped."

Tiffany MacMillan? That was Tiffany's nasally voice. Samara and Becca were pow-wowing about me with Tiffany?

"Well, it's more than that. We still don't know what really *happened* to her," Becca said.

"Why won't she tell you?" Tiffany said. "I thought you guys were like, besties."

"We are," Samara replied. "At least, we were."

Man, was there nothing else to talk about in Eastcove? Was I the only gossip worthy news?

I cleared my throat, and Samara and Becca turned sharply, both of them flushing an unpleasant red as they tried to compute what it was I might have heard.

I just marched past them to the hallway where a list told us whose homeroom we were in. Samara and Becca rushed in after me.

"Dori," Becca said. "We didn't *know* you were there."

Obviously. "Since when are you guys buds with Tiffany."

Samara folded her arms. "Well, it's not like you've been a blast to hang with lately."

Ouch. Painful but true.

"Look, I'm sorry," I started, hoping the water works wouldn't bubble up again. Even I was sick of them. "I've had a hard summer, but it's not your fault. I'm really going to try to snap out of it. Please, just be patient with me."

Samara unfolded her arms and Becca's face softened into a smile. "Of course, Dori," Becca said. "We're here for you."

Samara gave me a quick sideways hug and Becca sandwiched us together.

"Okay, enough of the love fest," Samara said tossing her black braid. "The bell's about to ring."

"Seaweed!"

I turned to find Colby leaning against a locker, a crooked grin on his face. Samara and Becca snuck me curious looks just before I went to him.

"Hey, Colby."

We'd held hands last night. Under the stars. Did he think it meant something more than I meant it to be?

"I'll walk you to your homeroom."

I couldn't very well say no, but to be honest I didn't want to. I liked Colby. I just didn't want to hold his hand in public. At least not yet. I hoped he didn't mind. I kept my arms tucked around my books.

I got my schedule in homeroom. First class? Earth science. Why was I taking this course again?

I took my usual seat at the front of the row. Now I was thankful I couldn't easily see Tor's old seat. Still, I couldn't stop myself from turning around for a peek. I could see him easily in my mind, sitting casually, a relaxed smile on his face and a glint in his too green eyes. I remembered how Tiffany flirted and made a fool of herself, but also how he'd still treated her with respect.

A lump formed in my throat and I forced a swallow. If I was going to survive this class, I couldn't keep doing that. Must get over Tor.

I turned to face the front of the room as Mr. Teaworthy walked in.

"Welcome to Earth Science 11," he said. "Today we're starting a study unit on the BP oil spill in the Gulf Coast. How it happened, the environmental and economical consequences, and what, if anything, can be done to prevent it from happening again."

Another oceanic natural disaster. I wondered if Tor had clan members down there, and if any of them had been caught in the sludge. Hopefully, they'd gotten away safely.

<h1 style="text-align:center">27</h1>

I'd survived the first morning of the first day of school. Now I just had to make it through the afternoon classes. I tried to keep my mind on the fact that Sidney was waiting for me to walk him to the park.

Samara and Becca were in another girl group huddle. The second one I'd caught them in, in one day. What was the deal with that? The happy buzz coming from them radiated in waves toward me, filling the hall.

"What's up?" I said. Samara and Becca looked kind of stricken when they saw me. "What?"

"Well," Samara started, "you know how they say lightening never strikes twice in the same place? It kinda did."

What was with the riddle? I opened my eyes wider in question.

Becca blurted, "There's another new guy!"

I gaped. "Okay. That is kind of weird, but not a miracle."

Becca gave me an apologetic look. "I think he's cute. I thought with what happened between you and..."

"That's fine," I cut her off before she mentioned Tor's

name. It hurt too much to hear it said aloud. "I mean that's great. I'm not interested anyway."

"And I'm happy with Mike," Samara added. I'd forgotten that she and Mike had gotten together over the summer. I hadn't even celebrated with her. I was such a loser friend.

Becca giggled like a little girl. I had yet to see this guy, so I wondered if she had a chance. I knew she was dying to get a boyfriend.

Suddenly a hush fell on the group.

Becca's face was beat red and her smile stretched wide across her face. I guessed the new guy was heading down the hall. The group of girls divided like the Red Sea, their bodies pressed up against the lockers as he sauntered by.

He was a little above average height with broad shoulders, but a slim, fit build. A swimmer's body? He had shaggy sandy-colored hair that almost touched his shoulders. And blue eyes. Almost too blue.

A shiver of nerves shot through my body.

It couldn't be.

Could it?

He kept his face down, his shy stance even more appealing to his audience.

Until he saw me.

His eyes connected with mine, intense and unsmiling, like I was the only girl in the hall.

Then he flashed a smile, turning on his heels to keep eye contact with me before the flow of the crowd forced him to break it.

"What was *that*?" Becca snapped.

"I don't know. I didn't do anything." My legs were shaking. "Like I said, I'm not interested and I mean it."

Becca stomped away, barely concealing a glare.

"Well, it seems you got the knack," Samara said before joining up with Mike and heading to her next class.

I didn't know if I had the knack. I only knew I wasn't happy with this new arrival.

In fact, I was a little scared.

28

*Y*ou never knew what kind of weather you were going to get in the Maritimes in the fall. Sometimes the snow was falling by the end of September. Sometimes we got an Indian summer that gave us the warmth of spring until mid-October or longer.

It looked like we were in for a nice warm one this year. And because of this, we were sitting outside, eating lunch and hanging out while we waited for the next bell to ring. I sat beside Samara, who was snuggling close to Mike. It was weird to see them all ga-ga like that when they literally had known each other forever, and I'd only ever seen them as friends.

Becca sat across from me, her eyes darting around the school yard, looking, I bet, for you-know-who. Colby shuttled in beside me. He raised his eyebrows wildly at Samara and Mike's ongoing PDA and I sent invisible vibes alerting him that he would have no such luck with me.

He got the hint and left a good six inches between us.

Tiffany sat at the next table where Sawyer was making an

effort to get her attention and affections. I'd say his efforts were hugely wasted.

Where was the new guy? Not that I cared, but I was curious.

"What's his name?" I said in Becca's direction.

"Uh, oh, who?" she said, like it wasn't obvious that her radar was on full alert for him. I tilted my head.

"Oh, him. His name is Ky."

"That new kid?" Colby said.

And just then, like mentioning his name produced him out of mid air, Ky strolled up and settled in beside Becca. Her whole body stiffened with excitement; her smile stretched broadly across her face.

Tone it down, girl.

"Hey," he said to us all. "I'm Ky Larson."

A round of "heys" went around the table. Ky sat with his shoulders back, his jaw relaxed and his eyelids light, like he hadn't a care in the world.

I didn't believe it for a minute. This was a guy on a mission.

"So, Ky," I said leaning forward across the table. "What brings you to Eastcove?"

He leaned forward, too, mimicking my stance, his eyes sparkling with flirtation. "Would you believe me if I said you?"

Becca and Colby choked on their sodas at the same time. If that wasn't brazen, I didn't know what was.

The thing was, I believed him.

"Why?"

"Why what?"

"Why did you come to Eastcove?" *I know who you are, buddy*. Or more like, what he was. But why was he here? Didn't he have some underwater battle to fight? I wished he'd take his jacket off so I could see his arms, check for telltale tattoos.

"Is there something wrong with Eastcove?" His eyes were

really, really blue. He leaned in a little more, like we were the only two people at the table. "I've only heard great things about it."

From who? Tor?

"Where are you living?" He better not be in Dex and Tor's cave.

He licked his lips evilly. "Why? Would you like to come over?"

"Hold on, here," Becca said. "Do you guys know each other?"

The whole table had stopped chatting. Colby threw me a questioning look.

"You guys *are* being kind of intense," Samara said.

"No," I said, when Ky didn't. "We don't know each other."

I turned to Colby. "Let's go."

He jumped up to follow me inside. When we got out of earshot he said sharply, "What was that about?"

I shook my head. It wasn't like I could tell him. It wasn't like I could tell anyone.

The rest of the afternoon crawled by at a snail's pace. My legs jumped with nervous energy as I watched the excruciating second hand of the clock tick throughout the last class.

I climbed into the front seat of the Rotten Apple in record time. Come on Luke! I just needed to get out of here. To get away from *him*. I'd manage to avoid another Ky sighting, and I didn't want to ruin my objective now.

I spotted Luke with Jolene, over by the playing field. His hands gestured, and his expression was animated in such a way I could tell he was in the middle of some story. I'd get home faster if I walked.

So, I did.

Sidney waited on the front steps.

"Hi, boy." I scrubbed his ears letting out a long breath. After I grabbed an apple, we headed out to the park.

I was glad that Colby had swim club because I wanted to be alone. I really needed to think.

If Ky was merfolk, what was he doing here? And why did he come alone? Or the bigger question, why didn't Tor come back, too?

Ky reminded me of Tor in his sleek look, flawless skin and too beautiful eyes. But in other ways, they were nothing alike. Tor never came on to me or anyone when he first arrived. Tor seemed to bring a sense of calm with him, where as Ky stirred up agitation.

I jogged the last bit of the distance to give Sidney a bit of a work out. He'd gotten a little chubby since my boycott of the beaches. I headed for the swings and fitted my butt into one, pushing my weight off the ground with my feet, falling into an easy rhythm.

Across the field was a sand pit. A couple young moms sat on a bench nearby, visiting as their little boys played. My mind went unbidden to the sand sculpture competition. I could see Tor's expression clearly; his brow furrowed in concentration as he formed my image. That was back in another lifetime when I wasn't yet a mermaid, when I didn't know about the clans, and when I didn't know what it felt like to fall in love.

Or to be crushed by rejection.

I'd only known Tor for a month. One measly month. That was all it took to wreck my life.

"Hello."

I jumped at the sound of his voice, bringing my swing to a stop. "Ky?"

"Small world."

Yeah, too small.

Sidney started whimpering and rushed to my side. I

scratched his ears, feeling déjà vu, remembering the first time Sidney and I came across Tor. Except that Tor had been singing in a way that drove canines crazy.

"Nice dog." Ky sat in the swing beside me. He waited a few seconds before continuing, "You know, I thought Eastcovers would be friendlier."

"We're friendly."

"Maybe I just hit a bad day."

I contemplated walking away, but then I'd just prove his point. And really, what did I have to gain by being a total jerk.

"Sorry, I know I was rude to you today. So, um, welcome to Eastcove."

"Thanks."

I couldn't help but dig. "I'm surprised we haven't heard anything about your family moving to town, because Eastcove is small. News like that usually gets around."

"My parents likes to cruise. We sail from port to port. We don't usually stay anywhere long enough to get to know people."

"And yet you came to school?"

"Homeschooling all the time can be very lonely. I like to meet people, even if I know I'm not staying long."

Did I read this guy wrong? Maybe I'd jumped to conclusions, just because he was new and good looking.

I watched him out of the corner of my eye. The sun was setting, casting a comforting warm glow. In this light Ky didn't look menacing at all. He looked like a normal guy. A normal *human* guy.

What an idiot I was. This whole thing with Tor had messed with my head.

"Can we start again?" I smiled sheepishly.

His grin widened. "Sure."

The moms gathered their kids and toys. Other people cut

through the park on their way to somewhere else. A couple of teens made out on a blanket on the lawn.

"Can I ask you something," Ky said.

"Shoot."

"Are you and that Colby guy together?

Yikes. Why would he ask me that?

"Um, not really, but we're good friends."

"So, I have a shot, then?"

I was so not used to the forwardness of this guy. "Well, actually, I just got out of a relationship, and I'm not really interested in getting involved again." Especially with someone who just told me he was only here for a short time.

But to make sure he understood, I added, "But if I did decide I was ready, I'd go out with Colby."

Ky nodded, and I thought he got the message. Until he said, "I guess I have my work cut out for me then."

THE NEXT MORNING I got up early. I walked Sidney, dressed and blow dried my hair. It was healthier now that I wasn't abusing it with chlorine; the blond was highlighted naturally from the sun, not a hint of green in sight. I brushed it until it shone and pulled it back into a ponytail.

I tried to see me the way Ky did. What was it that fascinated him so much? Sure, I was okay looking, and with makeup I could turn heads, but I wasn't exactly fashion runway material. There were a lot of girls more interesting to look at than me.

Maybe he was attracted to me because I so obviously shunned him. Some guys couldn't stand that. Ky seemed like the kind of guy with a larger than life ego.

I decided on a little mineral foundation to hide the circles under my eyes—I hadn't slept that well since.... well, let's just say, for most of the summer.

And a touch of lip gloss. That was it. I wasn't going to school to attract guys. Despite everything, I still wanted to get an education.

Surprise, surprise, Ky was at my locker when I got there, and Becca happened to arrive with me. She huffed down the hall before I could say anything.

I worked my lock combo. "Go away."

"Whoa, I take it you're not a morning person."

He looked great and smelled terrific. Why? Why couldn't he have bad breath or greasy hair?

"Look, Ky, I don't mind being friends, but there are people here, people I care about who wouldn't understand, so please, no stalking, okay?"

"I didn't take you for the kind who cared about what people thought?"

Was that a slam or a compliment?

"Well, I do today."

Of course, Colby would arrive while we're talking.

"Dori, is he bugging you?"

I stared pointedly at Ky. "No, we were just finishing up. Let's go." I walked with Colby to my homeroom, my arms tight around my binder. I couldn't help but sneak a peek behind me. Ky was smirking. I fumed. If he thought he was going to win this thing, whatever this thing was, he was wrong.

"I don't like that guy." The muscles in Colby's neck tightened as he talked. "I don't like how he looks at you, like you're a piece of steak and he hasn't eaten in weeks."

Really? That was what Colby saw?

"He's just lonely from all the traveling and homeschooling he does."

"You're defending him?"

Honestly, I thought Colby was going to burst a vein or something.

"I don't need to defend him. There's nothing going on between us, and I'm a big girl. I can take care of myself."

Thankfully, the bell went and Colby had to get to his own classroom. Really, I felt like the world had gone crazy. Some seam in the universe had ripped open and all common sense and normality had been shaken out like feathers. Nobody was who they used to be last year, it seemed. Especially me.

29

Ky's effort to win me over never let up as the days went on. He'd mysteriously show up as I walked to class, sat beside me through lunch and managed to get his seat moved next to mine in biology, the one class we had together.

I couldn't deny that I felt flattered by the attention, but there was a cost. Becca refused to talk to me, her last words being, "Why do you have to have all the good guys? Colby, and Tor and now Ky? You don't even want them. Can't you let me have a chance with just one?"

It hurt when she mentioned Tor, like I was the one who ended it there, but she didn't know the truth. Nobody knew.

And Colby was far from thrilled by Ky's appearances at the park. He'd show up every evening whether Colby was there or not. It wasn't like there were a ton of parks for me to choose from in Eastcove.

The whole thing was just out of control.

Colby's angst over the whole Ky thing had reached new levels.

"I just don't like the guy. He's pushy and... just always, there."

We sat on a bench by the sand pit which was currently void of kids. "I can't help where he chooses to hang out, Colby. Besides, he said he never stays anywhere long."

Colby reached over, stroking my cheek as he pushed a fly away strand of hair behind my ear. "It's just I think, if he hadn't come to Eastcove, you and I would be... further along."

He was probably right. Though, Ky wasn't Colby's only competition, not by a long shot. I still fell asleep every night thinking about Tor and spent most of it dreaming about him, too.

I gave Colby a gentle smile. "Be patient, okay."

I thought he would agree. His eyes had started to say yes, until he spotted something in the distance. Something that brought all that anger straight back to the surface.

I knew what he saw before I turned to follow his gaze. Ky's silhouette sauntered toward us in the dusk.

Colby shot to his feet. "Get lost, loser," he spit out.

Ky's confident grin never twitched. "Hey, it's a free country, last I'd checked. And I'd watch who you call a loser."

Colby practically snarled. "Is that a threat?"

"Colby," I said, sharply. Down boy.

Ky laughed. "Maybe." He removed his jacket and let it fall to the ground. "I can tell you've been itching to do this all week. Let's get it over with."

And that was it. Colby butted his head into Ky's chest, pushing him to the ground. I jumped onto the bench to get out of the way as they rolled on the grass. Colby was a star athlete, but Ky was no slouch.

Colby was on top. He punched Ky hard in the gut. I screamed. "Stop, it!"

They rolled again, now Ky was on top. His fist connected

with Colby's face. Colby cried out. I couldn't stand to see Colby hurt. I ran and jumped on top of Ky pulling on his shirt. "Get off him!"

I heard a rip. Ky's shirt. He heard it too, and jumped off Colby who writhed on the ground, his hands to his face.

Ky's eyes were hard. He glanced at the rip in his shirt and then fixed his sights on me. He knew I saw them. His tattoos. They were just like Tor's.

30

Ky stooped to pick up his jacket and trekked off into the darkness, like he hadn't just clobbered Colby.

I rushed to Colby's side. "Colby, are you okay? Colby?"

He let out a groan, water leaking from his eyes and down his face, blood draining from his nose. I had a tissue in my jacket pocket. I plucked it out and handed it to him.

"Is it broken?"

"I don't know. I don't think so. I'm gonna kill that S.O.B."

I didn't think Colby would be able to see him to kill him. His left eye was swelling shut, from what I could see in the street light.

I helped Colby up. At least his legs and arms were fine and he'd still be able to swim. "I'll walk you home," I said.

"No, that's okay. I can find my way."

"Are you sure?"

"I'm sure, okay?" It came out stronger than I thought he intended. I knew Colby well enough to know he was embarrassed. He'd lost a fight he had started.

I called Sidney who had gone into a barking fit during the fight. I was glad the park had been empty.

I had time now to think about what I'd seen. Ky had tattoos. Merfolk tattoos. I had been right with my original intuition.

That meant his story about cruising with his family and homeschooling was a lie. But why? Why wasn't he busy fighting the Lars clan with the rest of the Rai? Why was he here, with legs in Eastcove?

And what did he want from me?

I TOSSED and turned all night and almost decided to skip school. Too much drama. But my curiosity got the best of me. Would Ky show up? Would Colby?

I met up with Samara and Becca in the hallway.

"Hey," Samara said. Becca gave me a weak "hi" but she still insisted on nursing her grievance with me. Samara was Switzerland and had little patience for our nonsense as she saw it. "How's it going?"

I tackled my lock, my eyes sweeping side to side watching out for Ky or Colby. "Uh, okay." Should I tell them about the fight in the park? Becca would probably see that as them fighting over me, and get her knickers even more in a knot. Maybe they were fighting over me, or maybe they just needed to fight.

It didn't take me long to figure out that both guys opted out from school today. In a way, it was a big relief for me. I walked myself to my homeroom and sat through biology and algebra without the knowledge that one guy or the other was focusing on what I did. I laughed at a joke with Sawyer and teased Mike about his love affair with Samara when he went on and on about how hot dark women were.

I felt normal-ish. Almost like it use to be, pre-Tor.

My mood dropped. Why did I have to go and think about him? I was doing so well.

My last class before lunch was gym. Since the development of my tattoos, I had to be very careful about keeping them concealed. It meant waiting until all the other girls had finished changing and had left the locker room before throwing on our assigned gym T-shirts. They were gray with a black sea-lion embossed on the front and the words Eastcove Sea Lions printed in an arc above it.

I heard the last girl walk out the door and I was alone in the room. I whipped off my shirt, and lifted my gym shirt over my head.

I yelped. Tiffany MacMillan stood in front of me, her eyes wide in shock. She must've come in when the last girl had opened the door going out. I quickly pulled my shirt over my head.

"What happen to you?"

"Uh, what?"

"Are those bruises?"

She knew I wasn't the kind of girl who'd actually get real tattoos. "Yeah, it turns out I have this blood condition. I bruise really easily, but I'm on meds for it, so they should go away soon. You won't tell, will you?"

Tiffany's face broke into a conspirator's grin. If there was one thing Tiffany loved it was a secret.

"Sure, I'm cool."

She grabbed the water bottle she'd forgotten and left me to finish up. I went to the mirror and lifted my shirt. Green and blue swirls with hints of pink cupped my shoulders. In the water they were glossy, and shimmered in the sunlight.

Like Ky's, except a daintier version. I was more like him than I was like Colby. I could never swim with Colby again.

But I could with Ky. Maybe I *should* go out with him. He could take me swimming. He could protect me.

Something gurgled deep within my being. I could hear the ocean in my ears, throbbing, pulsating. It was a deep need like the need to eat or the need to breathe. I wanted to be in the sea. I needed to be.

I would go to Ky. Not as a girlfriend, but as a friend. I'd tell him I knew what he was and that I was like him. We could swim.

"Dori!" Tiffany shouted through the door. "Mr. Peters is popping screws waiting for you!"

I was so excited about the prospects of my new plan that I could barely stand waiting for the rest of the day to go by.

Plus, I'd forgotten that I didn't know where Ky lived. At the cave?

I waved goodbye to Samara and Becca, both waved back perplexed by my sudden good mood. I didn't even go home first. I went straight to the cave.

I'd hadn't been there since the middle of summer, and I stopped short when I came to the crevice. Was I ready to go back down there? To revisit the place where Tor and I had spent the night through the storm. The evening I'd realized I'd fallen in love. The last good memory I had of Tor?

I could hear the waves slapping the rocks and the desire to return to the sea overrode my sadness.

I found my footing and jumped the last foot onto the sand. I turned and stared at the cave. It looked dark and uninhabited.

"Ky?"

I proceeded cautiously, not entirely sure this was a great idea. Maybe Ky didn't know about this cave. Maybe some wacko had come across it from the land side and was squatting here.

I had to find out. "Ky?"

I got to the entrance. It was dark, but I could see light from the sky lights up ahead. My vision started to adjust to the dimness.

I stepped inside. "Ky?"

"Dori?"

It was a voice I recognized, but it wasn't Ky's.

It was Tor's.

31

I felt faint, like I didn't have enough blood. A hundred nights of dreaming about Tor never prepared me for actually seeing him in flesh and blood.

"T-tor?"

"Hi."

I didn't know what to do. The cot still sat up against the wall. I reached for it and sat. I was so stunned; I didn't know what to say. Plus my heartbeat had revved up to dangerous levels. I wanted to lie down, get my breath, but I still had a little pride.

"Are you okay?" Tor said, taking a step toward me.

"No. No I'm not." Now that my brain had time to process this new turn of events, my emotions caught up, too. Rage spewed out.

"What do you care? Why did you come back? I'm just getting use to you being gone. Why don't you just go jump back into the ocean where you belong?"

They were harsh, hateful words. A shadow of pain washed

across his face, his beautiful, perfect face, and I felt a stab of remorse.

"Let me explain, Dori, please." His voice was soft and lyrical. Despite my anger, it soothed me.

Besides, I was curious.

"You've got two minutes."

He sat beside me and I almost went crazy. His musky scent, his closeness, it made me wild. My heart was skipping all over the place and my nerves quivered. I wrapped my arms around my knees to keep them from shaking. I hated how he affected me and I didn't want him to know how destroyed I felt.

"It's Ky."

"What? You're here because of Ky? Why? You don't want me so that means no one else can?"

"No, that's not what I mean. You don't know what he is."

I had to laugh. A dry, crackly, totally unattractive laugh.

"What makes you think I don't know? What makes you think I even care? You know what, Tor Riley?" I stood up, indignant. "You had your chance and you blew it. If I want to hang out with Ky, I will and there's nothing you can do to stop me."

I stormed away, all drama-queen, really hoping that Tor wouldn't run after me. And really, really sad when he didn't.

32

*W*hy did I run off so soon?

A minute ago I was brimming with spew, wanting to hurt and maim Tor with my words. Now I desperately wanted to kiss him deeply.

I missed him. I still wanted him.

I was such a weakling.

Half way to town I collapsed on a knoll. I had a sliver view of the ocean and I focused on that sliver, guiding my breath. In. Out.

No. It was good that I ran. Kissing Tor would've been the absolute wrong thing to do. But I did wish I would've asked him more questions, like was he okay and was he with Shava, and had Kon forgiven him for bringing me to the Rai clan and was he with Shava, and had the Lars clan attacked and *was he with Shava?*

Freak. I couldn't believe I still didn't know this one important fact.

I stood, brushing the dirt and grass off my clothes, and headed back to Eastcove toward Main Street.

My mind raced, trying to figure out the puzzle. Why was Tor here and what did it really have to do with Ky?

I should've given Tor three minutes.

By the time I was half way down Main Street, past the town hall and police station, my heart had calmed. My anger and sadness were mixed up into one confused muck.

I had to get home to walk Sidney, and I had algebra homework to do. I should probably email Colby with the homework he missed.

Across the square I saw Nana outside of the produce market. She was examining the apples piled in a bin outside on the walk.

I stayed on my side of the street, my head down. I knew I had to talk with her about everything I knew one day, but I just wasn't up to it yet. My nerves were so frayed that I didn't think I could handle one new surprise.

Next to the produce store was a used book and magazine shop. A broad-shouldered man had a news magazine opened, covering half his face. His eyes peered over the top edge of the paper, so he obviously wasn't reading. He was spying. The only person in his line of vision that I could see was Nana.

I looked more closely. The man shifted. I recognized his build. Tall and solid. Long gray hair streamed out of the bottom of a green rain cap.

Dex?

Dex was spying on Nana?

Just a lonely old merman—or more?

A crack of thunder. Lightening jagged across the darkened brooding sky. Dex quickly put the magazine away and turned to head out of town. A rainstorm was brewing. Time for all good merfolk to get out of sight.

On the one evening I actually wanted to meet Ky at the park, we were both stuck inside.

. . .

THE NEXT MORNING, I really, really didn't want to go to school. What if all *three* of them showed up? Kill me now.

"Dori!" Mom called up from the bottom of the steps. "Are you up? Don't tell me I have to walk your dog again."

"Sorry," I shouted back. "Coming."

I'd fake being sick, but I hated getting behind in school. My grades were sucking as it was because of all these social messes I was in.

Mom took on dog duty after all, so I could catch my ride in the Rotten Apple. I didn't have time to primp and I was glad of it. Looking good was a liability in this situation. I couldn't fault Colby, but with Ky and Tor, their attraction was probably all just merfolk instinct or something equally questionable.

My strategy was to keep a low profile and avoid Colby and Ky as much as possible.

I waited in the Rotten Apple until the bell rang, then sprinted to my homeroom, not even stopping at my locker.

Samara mouthed, "You're late?" but I managed to get into my seat before Mrs. Henry looked up from her romance novel she didn't even try to hide that she was reading.

Mrs. Henry took attendance then went back to her book. She released us to get a head start toward our first class which was helpful to me because I still needed to get to my locker.

Samara walked with me. "Thank God it's Friday. Hey, Mike and I are hanging out at his place tonight. You could come."

Colby stood by my locker. I let out a defeated breath. Both of his eyes were black and blue.

"What happened to him?" she asked before I could respond to her invitation.

What could I say but the truth? "He got into a fight with Ky."

"Over you? Jeez, Dori."

"Not over me—over each other. Can't have two alpha males in a pack, that kind of thing."

"Stupid."

I agreed. "Hey, Colby."

"Seaweed."

Samara tagged him in the arm. "Nice shiners. How did the door make out?"

"Heh, heh," Colby said. "Have you seen him? I'm going to knock his block off."

I pulled my locker door open. "I think you should calm down, Colby. Fighting's not the answer."

My eyes darted around nervously. I really hoped Ky didn't show up this minute. I slammed my door and walked with Colby to algebra.

Next class was biology, then I would see Ky. I hated to admit it, but if Ky asked me to skip school with him this afternoon, I knew I'd say yes.

He was already in class when I got there. If Colby had injured him, you couldn't tell by looking. He shook his hair off his forehead when he saw me, an appreciative smile forming on his face.

I kept the glee I felt to myself, forcing a blank look. I couldn't allow him to think that beating Colby up was okay. Even if he had asked for it.

"Hey," he said as I sat down. I nodded and opened my books on my desk, pen and pencil ready, always the good student.

"Sorry, about the other night. I should've exercised some self-control."

He had his head tilted in that endearing way and it made it

hard to keep up my guise. His leg brushed against mine. On purpose? A little shiver shot up my back.

"But you have to admit, he's a jerk."

I tapped my pen on the desk. "Colby is an intense guy. You just have to get to know him."

"Uh, not interested."

"He's my friend, so if you want my forgiveness you have to be nice to him."

He flashed that crazy grin. "Wow, you drive a hard bargain. Okay, here's the deal. I'll be nice to him if you go out with me."

I dropped my pen on my desk and swallowed. "I told you. I just got out of a relationship." And the guy was back in town. "I'm not ready."

"Okay, not out, out, just out. As friends."

Now the pen was in my mouth. Gnaw, gnaw. Should I? What about Tor? What *about* Tor? Hanging out with Ky would help me forget him, which was exactly what I needed to do.

Plus, he would take me swimming, which was also what I needed to do.

I stalled. "Um, I don't know."

"I found this awesome little shack down by the ocean. It's a cool place to hang out."

The ocean. So far, so good.

"Yeah?"

"We could go swimming."

I looked at him pointedly. Nervous energy surged between us. I knew what he was saying. Did he know I knew? Did he know about me?

I finally said, "It's kind of cold for swimming, don't you think?"

"For some people."

He was testing me.

"But not you?" I queried.

"And not for you."

He did know about me. But how? Freak. He could probably *smell* me. That was why he came on so strong at the beginning.

We skipped out of the afternoon classes. The shack wasn't in walking distance so we borrowed Luke's dirt bike. I figured as long as we had it back before Luke was done with his shift at Joe's Garage, he'd never know. Ky wore Luke's helmet and I used the extra one he had for Jolene.

Normally, I'd never take something of Luke's without asking, but the urge to swim was too strong. Like a drug. I needed my fix. Today.

Faded blue paint peeled to reveal the gray worn wood of a small cabin. Long grass grew in tufts around its foundation and a cast iron table was chained to a hook cemented into a small patio. I frowned. It wasn't abandoned, it was locked up. For winter.

"This isn't an old shack, Ky. It's a cabin. Someone stays here in the summer."

Ky twisted off the padlock; it only looked like it had been locked. "I snipped it off last time," he said as he opened the door. "It's okay, Dori. We're just visiting. We're not hurting anyone. We'll leave it exactly the way we found it. No one will ever know."

I held back. "It doesn't feel right to me."

"What? You don't like breaking the law?"

"I try not to make a habit of it."

"But skipping school is fine."

"No, it's not fine. I don't usually skip school, just..." The ocean was only fifty feet away. I turned and stared at the foam as the waves lapped to shore, in and out like breath. The ocean lived. It breathed. Its rhythm called me.

The wind whipped along the sand, stirring up little tornado swirls. I wrapped my jacket tighter. The weather had cooled since the storm.

"C'mon, let's just warm up a little, then we can leave." Ky motioned with his hand and I reluctantly entered.

A dim afternoon light shone through low windows showcasing all the dust particles dancing in the room. The furniture had been stowed neat and tight against the walls. The small fridge was propped open, empty and unplugged. Two doors in the short hall were closed.

Suddenly I felt unsafe. I'd let myself be drawn away to a strange place with someone I hardly knew, leaving no word with anyone about where I had gone. I'd broken all the rules.

Ky leaned up against the counter. "What are you thinking, Dori?"

"What do you know about me?"

"What do you mean?"

"I saw your tattoos; you know I did."

"So, lots of guys have tattoos."

"Not like those."

Ky chuckled. "Okay. I have 'tattoos.' So do you."

"What else do you know about me? What are the Rai saying?"

Ky gave me a long look. "Well, you definitely are the talk of the undersea world, I'll give you that. You were a big surprise. A big, pleasant surprise."

What? I thought the Rai were *unpleasantly* surprised. A little red flag popped up in my head, but I couldn't place what was wrong.

Ky continued, "And I know you're dying to go swimming. So, let's go."

He was jittery, fidgeting with his fingers, tapping them on the countertop. Rat-a-tat-tat. Controlled excitement, like a kid nearing the end in a puzzle race, afraid the next guy was going to finish before he did.

Ky really wanted to go in the ocean, that was obvious, but he could do that any time. He didn't need me.

"You go first," I said.

"I'd rather we go in together."

"I'd rather not."

We were stalemated. All was silent, except for the thundering sound of the beat of my heart.

Then a knock at the door.

"Ky!" I whispered. I knew it. We'd been caught trespassing.

"It's okay. Just act like this we belong here." He moved to the door. "I'll get rid of them."

He opened the door, but the knocker wasn't into pleasantries. He kicked it wide open with his foot.

I screeched, "Tor!" What was *he* doing here?

Tor stepped into the space between me and Ky. "Get outside, Dori."

"What's going on, Tor? What's the matter with you?"

"Ky is Lars. He wants to take you to Prince Mol."

What? My brain couldn't compute. Ky was on land. I'd thought Lars couldn't get on land.

Before I had a chance to ask any more questions, Ky stormed into Tor, thrusting them both outside. They broke apart, each staring the other down like gunmen in an old western.

"We're on to you, Ky. You failed. Just go peacefully."

Ky shook his head. "I haven't failed yet." He pounced on Tor, grabbed him by the torso and flung him into the sky. Tor's body arched and landed with a thud in the hard sand, at least twenty feet away.

How'd Ky do that? His strength was inhuman. Of course, he *was* inhuman. But so was Tor. A fall like that would have seriously injured a regular guy, but it only stunned him for a couple seconds. Tor lifted himself up and brushed the sand off.

He yelled, "Run, Dori!"

Run where? Where could I go that either one of them couldn't find me. They both had extra-ordinary senses of smell, sight and intuition. I knew how mine had sharpened since becoming merfolk and I was half human. They were both fully merfolk.

Tor and Ky faced off like two wild animals. I realized now how much Ky had actually held back when Colby rushed him. Ky could've easily killed him without much effort, and I was suddenly overcome with the panic that follows an awareness of what could've happened.

Ky came in swinging his right fist, but Tor ducked it, then ducked it again. He punched Ky in the gut, a move that threw Ky backward ten feet.

They were hardly breathing heavy. I, on the other hand was hyperventilating on the verge of nervous breakdown.

Tor stepped up to Ky, who rolled away quickly on the ground, then sprung to his feet.

"She's mine, Tor. I will have her for my prince."

Oooh, creepy fear paralyzed me. I should've run when I had the chance.

"Not if I have anything to do about it."

Tor rushed Ky, grabbed his arm and started swinging him over his head. How was that possible? I'd never witnessed so much strength before. I was awed and dumbfounded.

Tor tossed him like a discus; Ky flew through the air, a shout escaping his lips. He landed in the ocean, sinking out of sight.

Tor reached for my hand. "Come on, we don't have much time."

Ky would have a tail by now, and I knew from experience that getting legs took more time than Ky would be willing to part with, not to mention he'd have to find a place more private than this.

"But, I don't get it," I said as we jogged away. "How is he Lars? He has legs."

"I'll explain it to you later."

We ran toward the dirt bike lying on the ground. I recognized it as Colby's. "You stole Colby's bike?"

"I didn't steal it. He lent it to me. I told him you were in trouble with Ky."

We didn't have helmets. Seemed today was a day of total recklessness. I held onto Tor's waist as he revved the bike and threw it into gear.

The wind filled my ears. My long hair blew behind me like a banner. I think I was in shock. I'd just witnessed the most amazing superhuman fight. Over me. I was with Tor again after a long summer of longing for him, holding onto his chest, my face pressed into his back.

I didn't know how it was possible, but Ky was Lars. He came to Eastcove to trick me into getting into the ocean, so he could give me to Prince Mol.

He very nearly succeeded.

I thought I might be sick.

33

We were losing daylight. I wanted to go home, but I didn't know if I'd be safe there. Tor must've had a destination in mind, as he kept us on a trail heading south.

Eventually he cut the engine. "We have to walk from here."

Walk where?

Tor tucked Colby's bike behind a bush, effectively concealing it. "Where are we going?"

"Just come with me." Tor headed toward the shoreline, pausing long enough to make sure I followed him. What else could I do at this point? Besides, now that we were together again, I wasn't in a big hurry to leave him. At least not without my questions answered.

The sun had disappeared down the western horizon a while ago and the residual sunlight faded into a deepening gray. Soon it would be dark.

When we reached the water's edge I could make out an object on the craggy beach. A rowboat.

"How did that get there?" I said.

"Uncle Dex arranged it."

"Where is he now?"

"He had to go back."

Before I had a chance to ask why, Tor was helping me into the boat. He pushed it into the bay, hopping in before getting his feet wet.

He took the paddles and began rowing.

The sliver-thin moon high in the sky didn't shed much light, and after a while a mass of clouds blocked even that.

The quiet and calm and seclusion of darkness settled my nerves. I felt like I could breathe again.

Tor watched me but didn't say anything, just rowed, the soft slap of the oars on the water surface creating a sense of time and space. We were moving, but I didn't know where to.

"Thank you," I said, finally. The weight of what had happened settled firmly in my chest, and the thought of how close I had been to being captured for Prince Mol made me shiver.

Tor simply said, "You're welcome."

I didn't know what else to say. Our voices echoed over the water, and I instinctively knew it was imperative that we remain silent, especially since we were passing the West Quoddy lighthouse. Its distinctive red and white horizontal stripes flashed with each blast of light, which meant we'd just crossed into waters belonging to the United States of America off the coast of Maine.

Dex had thought ahead to store bottled water on the boat along with a small cooler with food.

I couldn't stomach anything to eat at the moment, but I was grateful for water to drink and finished an entire bottle.

I blew out a heavy breath. My family. They were probably

freaking by now, with me not coming home by nightfall. They were going to go crazy with worry again and I felt terrible.

After awhile Tor brought us to shore.

"Quoddy Head State Park?"

He muttered, "Yes."

Quoddy Head was big enough and solitary enough, especially at this time of year, to hide a couple runaways. Tor surprised me when he pulled a pup tent out of a bag. I hadn't even seen it tucked away in the rowboat.

"We're spending the night here?"

Tor nodded, but abandoned tent building temporarily to build a fire.

I still couldn't believe I was alone with Tor, much less even deal with the idea of spending the night here with him. I snapped out of my state of shock enough to assist with the fire by gathering dried twigs and broken bits of fallen logs.

The cooler contained fish, cod mostly. I shouldn't have been surprised.

"Cooked?" Tor asked.

"If you don't mind." Raw fish didn't have the same appeal when I was in my human form.

Tor cleaned a branch with a jackknife, also stored in the boat, and speared a filet with it. He crouched while holding it over the fire. I was mesmerized by the glow of the firelight on his face, the intensity and determination of his expression as the shadows flickered across it.

It reminded me of the bonfire where we first met, and how I'd caught a glimpse of his face on the other side of the flames. And how that night, when he'd dived in to the ocean and I'd thought that he'd drowned, had changed everything.

"I can do that," I said.

Tor handed the branch with my meal speared onto it to me.

His palm brushed across my hand and I froze. He did, too, and when our eyes met I thought he might bend down and kiss me. My heart rocketed into my throat.

But he pulled back, a hint of sadness in his eyes.

Why? Was it Shava? Was he with her again?

Tor ate his fish raw. I flipped my meal over to be licked by the flames when one side was done. The aroma of it cooking set my hunger alight. I satisfied myself, picking the cooked flesh off the stick with my fingers.

Tor stared at me the whole time. He didn't even try to hide it. I couldn't wait any longer, I had to know.

"How's Shava?"

If Tor was surprised by my question, he didn't show it.

"She's fine."

Fine? What did that mean?

"Okay, let me spell it out. Are you and Shava back together?"

A beat. Tor leaned forward slightly. "No."

No? Really? So, how did that make me feel? He'd left me back in July and didn't come again until I was in danger. He still didn't want *me*. He just didn't want Prince Mol to have me, a decision I was in full agreement with.

"How can Ky be Lars? He obviously can come ashore."

"His father is Rai. His mother raised him Lars, but genetically, he took after his father. When Ky's mother died, he searched for his father among the Rai, but his father wouldn't acknowledge him. Mating between the clans is forbidden, and he refused to admit that he had violated the law.

"Ky happened to be at the age of choosing. With his Rai genes, he was an anomaly among the Lars. He realigned himself with them, and Prince Mol demanded that he go to shore, as a test to see if he could. Unfortunately, it worked."

"So couldn't Ky perpetuate the Rai quality among the Lars clan?"

Tor shrugged. "His offspring would be only quarter Rai. We don't know. But Prince Mol's ego wouldn't let Ky have the distinction of fathering a new clan of land-dwellers, when there's a possibility that he could do it.

"As a subject of the prince's, Ky would never trespass Mol by trying. Not unless Prince Mol's efforts fail and he was personally ordered to by the prince.

"Either way, Ky is the first Lars able to work for them out of the sea. Because of this, he's very, very dangerous."

"But I thought Shava had a parent from each clan."

"Yes, but this is not a well-known fact. Her mother is my aunt, the queen's sister. My aunt was a rebel, some say unstable. She flirted with the other side, and Shava was a result. No one knows who her father is."

"This unfortunate circumstance never kept you from loving Shava?"

"No, it's not her fault who her parents are. She's still my cousin."

Right.

Now that my stomach was full and my burning questions answered, my primal need perked up. The ocean seemed to tease me with the slapping of the waves up against the rocks, spraying mist into the air. I could smell it. I wanted it.

"Take me swimming, Tor."

"Absolutely not."

"Please, just a short swim. It's been so long."

"It's not safe."

"How so? No one knows we're here. *I* barely know where we are. It's dark. The satellites can't even see us. Please, Tor? Imagine if you hadn't been in the ocean for two months." I didn't add that he was the reason for my aquatic exile, but he knew that already.

Quiet. He was thinking. Hope spurred me on. "Remember the fireworks?"

"How could I forget?"

The fire before us snapped. Something else was snapping, too, an energy and desire that both Tor and I shared.

"I missed you," he said.

"But you left me."

"It was a sacrifice."

"Who asked you to make it?"

"No one."

"Then I can hardly feel sorry for you."

His jaw tightened. I'd hurt him, but he'd hurt me. We hurt each other.

"You do remember what you have to go through when you come out?"

I did, but I couldn't think about that right now. I just shrugged.

Tor stood up. "Okay."

"Okay?" Yes! I couldn't believe it was finally happening. I rushed to my feet. Blood pounding, I felt light headed.

"Dori?"

"I'm ready."

"I'll go first."

I turned as Tor removed his clothes and waited until I heard a faint splash. I threw off my jeans and jacket, hardly concerned about my modesty in this darkness and ran into the ocean. I felt giddy like a little girl.

I gasped at first with the cold, but welcomed the wetness like an old friend. My legs began to tingle and stiffen until finally, a tail.

I slapped the surface with my tail fin and propelled myself

underneath. My gills activated and an eruption of bubbles encircled my head. I thrust myself deeper into the ocean. I could *see*, I could *hear*, I felt completely free. It was a rush and a high, and I loved it.

Dori?

He spoke to me. Through his thoughts. It felt like an eternity since I'd heard him call my name this way, so clearly, so deeply, so intimately.

Even in the darkness of night he shimmered, his tattoos dancing, his eyes like deep emeralds, his tail strong and feral.

The last time we swam together we had been a couple. We'd kissed like crazy people. We held hands as Tor pulled me into the depths of the sea. I'd discovered a fear of claustrophobia I didn't know I'd had.

I'd met his family, the king and queen and Tor's brother, Kon, and they had rejected me. I upset the clan equilibrium.

Crazy Jim Macdonald shot me. Tor rescued me.

And I fell in love.

I hadn't fallen out.

Tor could break my heart, over and over again, and I was completely helpless to stop him.

I had to swim away. Keep my distance.

Dori?

Instead of saying thank you I said, *I'm fine. Please just leave me alone.*

In an instant he was in front of me, his eyes level with mine. *We have to get out.*

Already? I need a little more time.

We can't. They're here.

Who? I'd been so introspective, that I'd completely tuned out my surroundings, but now I could sense something. *Them.*

The Lars must have spies watching the coast.

Oh, no. I'd put myself in danger again. Put us both in danger.

We headed toward the shore as fast as we could but it was too late.

Flashes of red. A dozen merfolk from the clan of Lars materialized, their tails gyrating at high speeds.

We were surrounded.

34

———

One of the Lars handcuffed my right arm to Tor's left with a rusty unit that must've bound prisoners a century ago. A rope that looked like it was made from seaweed was looped around my neck and held by a Lars like a leash. They assumed, and with some accuracy I thought, that Tor wouldn't try to escape if there was a chance I would be injured in his attempt. They carried rusty knives and swords, the kind you'd imagine pirates from old would carry.

Merfolk were expert swimmers, and though I knew I was propelling through the ocean faster than I'd ever swam before, I could still feel the tug and tightening on my neck. I gagged in reflex.

Slow down! You're hurting her.

One of the Lars flashed a look that said who cares.

Tor answered, *I'm sure the prince does.*

This must've been true, since the Lars did slow down a bit.

Eventually, I saw a large dark mass partially submerged on the sea floor. A sunken ship. The three bar rail that surrounded the deck was draped with green slime. The cockpit was intact, the door wide open; a single mast remained upright with green goo stringing off it. Along the sides of the vessel was a row of small black windows grouped in twos, like eyes.

Red patches of rust blended in with the washed out whites and blues of sea barnacles, and miniature crustaceans covered the surface.

The Lars pushed us into the cockpit. They untied the rope from around my neck, but left our wrists bound. The Lars disappeared through the door, easing it closed behind them.

My eyes quickly adjusted to the darkness. I was just grateful that the Lars hadn't taken us to a deep cave. Though my chest felt tight I hadn't hit the point of panic yet.

Are you okay?

Yeah, I think so. Where are we?

I'm guessing a few miles off the coast of Cutler. I can hear the Atlantic Puffin colony on Machias Seal Island.

I focused on the sounds coming from above. I could hear loud chirping resonating through the water. Atlantic Puffin reminded me of a cross between a penguin and a parrot. As if to prove our assessment was right, a Puffin dove past the small window in search of its next meal.

Have you been here before?

Uncle Dex and I lived near Cutler before we came to Eastcove.

Why did you leave?

The Lars showed up. We were uncomfortable with their numbers.

Red tail fins flashed past the windows, reminding me that we were indeed being held captive.

Why are there so many Lars?

Tor huffed. *The Lars aren't monogamous like the Rai. Their mermen have multiple wives and therefore more offspring.*

Tor rested his face in his free hand. *I'm so sorry, Dori. I wasn't careful enough. I failed you.*

It's not your fault. I'm the one who insisted we go swimming. I would've gone in with or without you; I wanted it that badly. I stroked his hand and he offered me a sad smile.

We infringed on the personal space of a squid squished into a corner and a nest of lobsters along the far wall. Tor and I pressed into an unoccupied nook and I took extreme comfort in feeling his shoulder rub up against mine.

What's going to happen now?

A stream of bubbles blasted out of his gills. *I'm not sure. Probably nothing until morning. We should get some sleep.*

Easier said than done. After this crazy day, I didn't think I'd ever sleep again, but then I did.

In the morning I could see light stream through the cracks in the seams of the ship and through the tiny windows.

My arm was asleep. Probably because it was positioned upwards at a forty-five degree angle, still attached to Tor's arm at the other end. His neck craned as he tried to see out the window.

Tor?

Oh, sorry, I didn't mean to wake you.

He swam back and I rubbed the circulation back into my arm. My chest still complained, the tightness growing, but my stomach was yelling the loudest.

I'm hungry.

Me, too.

Tor stared off into the corner. I followed his gaze. The squid?

Normally, when I was on land and had legs, the idea of eating raw squid would make me squirm, but right now, in my mermaid form, fresh raw squid would make my day.

Tor motioned for me to follow him slowly. I held back as

much as I could with my arm attached to Tor's, not wanting to get in the way. I certainly hadn't developed any underwater, weapons-free hunting skills. Tor became statuesque in his stillness. I held my breath. Then in a blink of an eye, Tor snatched it, ripping it apart in the middle.

I didn't like seeing it die, but I had no problem receiving a tentacle when Tor handed it to me, and I chewed it like it was candy.

It's obvious I would starve if I were down here without you.

I meant it as a thank you but Tor took it another way.

If I'd done my job, you wouldn't be down here at all.

I wanted to say something that would make him feel better. I hated the guilt he was carrying when we were really in this mess because of my own foolish impulses, but before I could come up with something intelligent, the door to the cockpit swung open.

Ky swam in with two henchmen on either side.

It was so odd to see him in merfolk form. His tattoos swirled wildly, his blond hair like a faux halo on his head and his tail, red with glints of blue and pink.

Wow, Dori, you make a hot mermaid. Prince Mol will be duly impressed.

Creep.

And Tor Riley, prince of Rai, as well. Bonus. The day couldn't get better.

I felt panic rise in my chest. Even though I was breathing fine with my gills, I suddenly really wanted to breathe with my lungs. Tor saw that I was in trouble.

We need to take her to the surface, Ky.

Why? She has gills. We have to get going.

She's not fully merfolk. Her body isn't used to being submerged.

Ky's mouth twisted as he contemplated Tor's request. His

face was drawn and narrow, like a rat. I really wondered how I'd ever thought he was good looking.

Getting me to Prince Mol in prime condition seemed to trump Ky's urgency to get me to him in a hurry.

All right. But no funny business. I may not want to harm the girl, but I have no qualms about letting her watch me kill you.

You stay under the surface!

Tor obeyed Ky's command as I broke water and sucked in a huge breath. It was weird to watch Tor's face distorted by the motion of the water looking up at me. However, Ky had surfaced and watched me with amusement.

"Wow, a real half-breed."

"I hear you're a half-breed yourself."

He tossed his head back slightly, as if he were surprised that I knew.

"Yeah, I guess I'm kind of a big deal. But you, I don't think you understand just what a big deal *you* are, Dori Seward."

"I think I get it, Ky. I'm not stupid."

"Well, except for your insistence to swim when you know you're being hunted by merfolk."

"Thanks for pointing out the obvious." My heart jumped a bit at the word "hunted". "I just can't believe I thought you were my friend." I couldn't believe I'd actually thought he *liked* me. "You really had me going there for a while."

"Deception in this case was a necessary evil."

Evil.

I hadn't been smart enough to be truly afraid of Ky before. My blood felt thick and slow. I was afraid of him now.

"Let's go." He dove and I followed. Tor shot me a worried look. I knew he'd heard everything we had said above the surface. My chills grew colder. Tor was afraid, too and that made me doubly afraid.

Ky and his peons with their archaic weapons pushed us into deep ocean. I told myself I could do this. I was acclimatizing. I might only be part merfolk, but I *was* part merfolk. I wouldn't give Ky the pleasure by freaking out about my lungs again.

The undersea world was kind of noisy. Sound traveled on water waves and I could pick up boat motors, whale calls, the crash of waves onto shore and just what I considered the pulsating breath of the ocean. It would be beautiful if my life weren't in danger.

I had an idea where we were headed because I'd Google Earthed the underwater mountain ranges after my last trek. There was one not far from the Maine/New Brunswick border. The closest peak just past the Fundian Valley was called Bear Seamount.

This journey gave me time to think about my family, and how they must be completely undone with worry. By now they'd know that I'd left school at noon yesterday. Colby knew I was in trouble with Ky: he believed Tor enough to lend him his bike. I was sure he'd told my parents everything by now. And probably the police.

I failed to tell Samara or Becca when I left, in truth because I was ashamed to be skipping out and I knew how Becca felt about Ky.

Boy, was she wrong about him. We all were. But to them, it

was just me, their unreliable BFF blowing them off again. I wondered if they'd be worried about this second disappearance or just plain mad. And what on Earth would I tell them if I did make it back home?

Oh no, not IF. I had to make it home. Somehow.

Tor had a sense for when my heart rate sped up. Even though our wrists were cuffed together, we'd managed so far to keep our hands to ourselves. Tor weaved his fingers through mine, and I didn't mind at all. I held on tight.

It turned out I was wrong about Bear Mountain. We skirted around the seamounts until we came to another sunken object submerged in the silty floor.

What is that?

Tor answered, *a German U-boat, U-856.*

A submarine?

I took it that while Rai preferred cave dwelling, the Lars liked to hang out in sunken ships. I'd bet they had a blast with the Titanic.

It was super eerie. In no way did I want to go in that rusted metal tube, with who knew how many skeletons of people who'd died in this battle.

The leading Lars opened a metal door and Ky ushered us in. He led us down a dark, narrow hallway until we came to the room he was looking for. There were a number of metal slats attached to the walls where mattresses once made a comfortable space for sleeping.

I gripped Tor's hand tightly. *It's worse than a haunted house.*

I imagined Germans sleeping in these bunks. How they dreamed at night of winning the war and about the terror they must've felt when they lost this battle and knew they were about to drown. It gave me the shivers.

I'm tired, I said, *please let's lie down and rest.*

We lay down on one of the slats. Tor put his free arm around me and I pressed my back into his chest like old times. I knew it didn't mean we were back together. I wanted Tor's comfort to help me to forget that we were in this nightmare. I think he wanted mine, too.

Tor had been so quiet since our capture. *What are you thinking?*

I'm trying to figure out a way to escape.

Will someone from Rai help us?

They will do something. I don't know what. They don't want to start a war, but they won't just sit around and let Prince Mol take you.

That brought me some comfort.

And they must want to save you as well.

Yes, they probably know by now that I failed at my mission.

The door opened. We sprung upright.

A swath of red hair. Shava!

Hello.

Not exactly the type of Rai help I was hoping for. Did she see Tor holding me close?

Shava? Tor swam to her. He'd forgotten that I was attached and I resented the jerk to my arm and being forced to greet her. Thankfully, he didn't kiss her.

Are you okay? he asked her. *How did they capture you?*

Oh, but I'm not a prisoner, Tor.

Tor's eyelids fluttered in confusion. *Then why are you here?*

The door opened again. Ky. Great. Why didn't we just have a big party while we were at it?

The surprises didn't end there. Ky swam up to Shava and put his arm around her shoulder.

Oh, you've got to be kidding, I said. *Are you together?*

Shava laughed. Hysterically. *Yes, we are. Tor you blew it. I'm done waiting for you.*

But he's Lars! he said.

She didn't blink. *And I'm Lars.*

Tor's jaw dropped like he'd been slapped. *You're defecting?*

I never really belonged with the Rai anyway. I always felt "less-than" because of my Lars father. If it hadn't been for my mother's royal connections, I would've been outcast long ago.

Your family cares about you, Shava. Think about what you're doing.

But do you care, Tor?

Of course.

Not enough to leave her.

I can't leave her here, Shava, you must know that.

I don't just mean leave her here. I mean leave *her.*

Tor didn't answer right away.

I told you Shava, Ky said, a slimy smirk on his face. *You are Lars. You belong here, with me.*

Shava's face hardened. The door opened and she followed Ky out without looking back.

I followed Tor around the room (had to) while he scrounged around for something that could unlock our cuffs.

We only got through half of the built-in drawers before the door opened again. Two large Lars swam in, followed by a beefy male Lars. He was the Schwarzenegger version of Lars with chiseled biceps and pecs. He had thick curly black hair like an inky mop and his eyes were more yellow than brown. If it weren't for his thick bright red tail, I'd have thought a demon just entered the room. Maybe one did.

As it was, his presence completely freaked me out because I knew who he was long before one of his guards announced him. Prince Mol.

Oh, help me.

I reached for Tor.

Which was the absolute wrong thing to do.

Prince Mol bellowed, *Don't touch him!*

I pulled away. Fortunately there was about two feet of chain linking us. I pulled as far away from Tor as possible.

Prince Mol swam around me and I could feel his eyes scanning my body. I couldn't stop quivering.

So this is the girl, he said. *Nice. I'm happy to have another wife, and this one is not only beautiful she will produce for me beautiful Lars children with the blessing of Rai.*

Another wife?

He stopped in front of me and stared meaningfully into my eyes. *You, my dear are the hope of the future.*

He cackled ridiculously, like he'd just told the funniest joke. His guards joined in. Then just as suddenly he stopped. To Tor he said, *We will see who has the blessing in the end.*

And to me, *Yes , my lovely, we will have a big wedding, a spectacle. The Rai will cry of course, but we will celebrate lavishly.*

Again his eyes landed on Tor. *Prince of Rai, you will be released. We want the girl, but we don't want a war.*

Please, Tor said, *might I request some time to say goodbye.*

The prince cackled again. *Why not? Let it be known that Prince Mol is capable of mercy.*

The instant Prince Mol was gone, Tor got frantic. We continued searching through the remaining drawers desperate for something that might help us. I spotted a thin rusty blade.

Tor, here's something. I think it was once a nail file.

Let me see it.

Tor worked our cuff with the file and I grimaced as it tugged at my skin. I thought the edge of the cuff might draw blood, but then suddenly, it snapped.

We were free, from each other anyway, and part of me wasn't exactly happy about that.

We'll keep the cuffs on, Tor said, *unlocked and keep them believing that we're still bound together. It might give us an edge.*

36

*O*ur current prison cell was devoid of squid and lobster or other aquatic squatters. Also of windows through which fish could swim. I was hungry again.

Do they plan on letting us starve to death? I held my stomach with my free hand for emphasis.

I'm sure they don't mind letting us get uncomfortable, but I highly doubt they'll let us starve.

As if they could hear us complaining (maybe they could? I hoped not!), the door swung open.

Ky swam in, a halibut in each hand. How nice.

Tor and I stayed closed together, as if our cuffs were secure. We accepted the fish with our free hands and ate greedily.

I understand you had your first meeting with your future husband, Ky said, clearly mocking me. *I think you will be very happy here, Dori. So sorry to see you go, Tor. The guards wait outside to release you.*

Tor gave me a sideways glance. I didn't know what Tor could do to Ky, but I knew I had to distract him somehow.

I swam so I was positioned closely in front of him keeping

eye contact. *Actually, Ky, I'm impressed with Prince Mol. I'd expected someone, you know, old, fat and bald, but he's really quite handsome.* If you liked guys with yellow eyes and red tails.

Ky's eyebrows shot up. Not the response he was expecting. He didn't have a chance to retort, though. While Ky was checking me out, Tor slipped out of the cuff and moved stealthily behind Ky. He wrapped the loose chain from our cuffs around Ky's neck and pulled until Ky's eyes crossed and he slipped to the floor like a doll whose batteries had been turned off.

Good work, Tor said. *I do hope you were only kidding, though.*

He tried the door. *It's locked.*

All my hope flitted to the ground along with Ky. Who by the way, wouldn't stay passed out forever. Unless he was...dead?

What are we going to do now?

The door handle vibrated. Someone was trying to get in, but whoever it was obviously didn't have a key.

Get behind me, Dori.

I did as Tor asked, holding on to his back. My heart raced. How were we going to deal with whatever was about to come through that door?

The knob continued to shake until eventually the door slowly opened.

There was no one there. I questioned Tor but he just shook his head.

Down here.

A mass of seaweed swirled around on the floor. I stared more closely. A head the shape of a small dragon popped up.

Barnaculoese!

Tor and I both shot over to him. If I'd known how to safely hug a sea-nymph, I would've.

Come, we don't have much time.

We followed Barnaculoese down the hall. Two Lars guards were incapacitated on the floor.

How? I asked Tor.

Barnaculoese has a powerful sting. Good to know.

The little sea-nymph must've spent some time scouting the place out with his terrific seaweed disguise, since he seemed to know exactly where to go. He stuck to the shadows, and we slipped behind other Lars who obviously didn't understand the strategic mind of the Rai or their sea world alliances.

We made it to an alternate exit, a window opening large enough for me and Tor to squeeze through.

You first, Princess, Barnaculoese said.

Princess?

Why'd you call me princess? I asked Barnaculoese once we were all out of the submarine and a good distance away.

When he didn't answer, I asked Tor. *Why did he call me princess?* A joke? Because I was almost forced to marry a prince? Not funny.

We can talk about this later. We need to get you to a safe place.

Soon other Rai joined us, as protection, I supposed I didn't feel like talking with them around. As I expected, we swam toward the seamounts and into a cave when we reached the closest one.

As soon as I entered the cavernous space, my heart began to race. I was okay with rooms in ships, I guessed because they were like rooms in houses, but caves were like tunnels, which I Did. Not. Like.

The way my chest tightened and my breathing accelerated,

I felt faint. I almost wished I were a Lars, if it weren't for all that other unsavory stuff.

Dori?

I just need a minute. I really don't like caves.

Okay, I'll help you breathe. Look in my eyes.

I focused on his eyes. The deep set green eyes that had turned my life upside down. His face was gentle and kind and the way he helped me calm my breath was so caring.

And he'd just saved my life again. I wanted to throw my arms around him and kiss him.

But that would be humiliating, because he didn't feel that way about me. Not anymore. I was important because of how I could personally upset the clan balance by bringing the Rai blessing to the clan of Lars should they succeed in capturing me.

I'd escaped this time, but it wasn't the last I'd see of them, I was sure. I'd be on the run from them for the rest of my life now.

Dori?

Yeah, I'm good. Just exhausted. Can I sleep somewhere? I remembered how Shava just closed her eyes while suspended in one spot. That wasn't what I meant. *Private?*

Tor showed me a ledge, similar to the one I tried to sleep on the last time, and instructed the Rai guards to give us some space.

Do you want to be alone?

No. Please stay.

Tor nestled in behind me, pulling my back to his chest.

Is this okay?

Yes. I let out a long breath. Yes, it was great.

Our breathing fell into a comfortable rhythm.

Tor, I finally asked, *why did Barnaculoese call me princess?*

He didn't seem like the kind of creature to make jokes, and something was twigging me.

Tor sighed. *Because you are. Uncle Dex is your grandfather. You are the heir to the throne of the clan of Rai.*

What??? Did I miss something here?

I turned to face him.

You're not making sense. Are you saying Dex and... my Nana?

Yes.

Oh, man. That was why Dex was spying on Nana. He still had a thing for her.

I thought you said you didn't know who my mother's biological father was?

I wasn't sure at the time, but I had my suspicions and Uncle Dex confirmed it.

And you're only just telling me this now?

I haven't really had a good opportunity.

I wasn't sure I agreed with that, but I let it go.

So, how does that make me a princess? Isn't your dad the king?

Before Uncle Dex met your Nana, he was the king. When he thought he was going to live a divided life on land with your Nana, he abdicated the throne to his younger brother, my dad. He didn't feel he could properly rule Rai while making a second life on land.

So this was why the king and queen had bowed to Dex.

Unfortunately for Uncle Dex, your Nana broke it off. She had her own choice to make, a normal life with her human family or one where her husband had another world and family under the sea that she could never be a part of.

Tor squeezed my hand and continued, *I don't think either of them knew there was a child on the way when they said good-bye.*

I could imagine the heartache they endured and for the first time, felt a little sympathy for my nana.

So now your dad has abdicated the throne back to Dex?

Yes. Father didn't feel fit to deal with the current unrest between the clans and the threat of war. Uncle Dex is better suited for the role and the clan has grown stronger since he stepped back into the rule.

How does Kon feel about losing his inheritance? Especially to me?

Obviously, he's not crazy about it, but it's out of his hands. Uncle Dex is the right man for the job.

Uncle Dex. My grandfather.

Hey, if Dex is your uncle and my grandfather, what does that make us?

Tor's mouth pulled up crookedly in a mischievous grin. *Cousins. Make that second cousins.*

Then he kissed me.

37

So we were cousins, so what? It wasn't like we were first cousins; we were *second* cousins. It wasn't illegal to date a second cousin, under the sea or above it, it was just weird. It'd be different if Tor and I had grown up together like siblings. If he'd seen me in diapers or something. Come to think of it, Colby and I have seen each other in diapers. Wouldn't it be weirder if I dated him?

Colby. I wondered how he was, if he'd even talk to me again when I got home, because that was exactly where I was headed.

Tor convinced me that Eastcove was the safest place for me right now, and actually, I believed him. I was in no hurry to meet up with Prince Mol again in this lifetime.

Or Ky Larson for that matter.

We were almost home, I could sense it. Tor had my hand and we were surrounded by a troop of Rai. No way the Lars could break through their ranks and snatch me.

Tor prepped me. *Tell them you skipped out of school to go dirt biking with Ky and that you got lost. When they ask what happened to Ky, tell them he dropped you off but was too embar-rassed to stick around and take responsibility.*

Let Ky take the fall?

Why not?

Good point. But, I was the one who took Luke's bike. I'll be grounded for sure.

And you skipped school.

Ugg. I see detentions in my future.

Tor laughed. *At least I'll know where to find you.*

Ha Ha. But what about Luke's bike. I'm assuming it's still at the cabin. Luke's going to kill me.

I'll pick it up and take it to your house before you return home.

I sensed that we were nearing the cave. I still didn't know what Tor was going to do next.

Will you stay with me?

I have to get the bike and get you settled.

I squeezed his hand. *No, will you stay with me, in Eastcove?*

You mean, go back to school and deal with all your moody friends?

Uh, yeah?

Your parents won't let you near another boy, you know. What chance do I have?

They'll get over this eventually. It's not like they can keep me from dating again in my lifetime

He squeezed my hand back. *Okay, you talked me into it.*

We stayed fully submerged until we reached the cave.

I'll go first, Tor said. The thought of being left alone in the ocean, despite the myriad of Rai strangers, left me feeling fragile.

I won't be long, and then I can help you.

He pressed his lips against mine, salty warm kisses to give me strength. Then he hopped out of the water.

I glanced around at the Rai surrounding me. Some of them had their eyes set on me, others with their backs toward me, keeping an eye out for intruders. I'd never felt so protected before. I'd never needed protecting. It was a strange feeling.

My guts squeezed as I thought of the pain I was about to endure. This was the cost of life as a Rai. If I wanted to be part of both worlds, and if I wanted Tor, and I did, I had to accept this.

Tor called me and I stuck my head out of the water, drinking in the fresh air. He took my hand and pulled me onto the rock.

He wore the jeans and T-shirt he kept hidden in the rocks. In his free hand he held a blanket; he must've made a quick trip to the cave.

He lay down beside me on the hard rock, his legs against my tail and threw the blanket over us.

In moments I felt the tearing, pulling, squeezing pain as my tail transformed into legs. I held on to Tor, squeezing his shoulders tightly. I couldn't help but cry out in pain, my mouth pressed to his chest. Tor stroked my hair and whispered in my ear.

"It's almost over."

Then as quickly as the pain started it ended. I let out a relieved breath. It was getting a bit easier each time.

"I don't have any clothes."

Tor scooped me up into his arms, just like last time, and carried me up the rocks. Leaves had started to fall and the wind blew them across our path. I shivered.

We ducked into the cave and Tor carefully set me down on the cot. "I'll be back as soon as I can. Just wait here, okay?"

"Okay."

Tor left and I wrapped the blanket tightly around my damp body. My eyes took in the empty cave. Besides the time I went searching for Ky, the last time I'd been here with Tor was the night of the storm. The night I'd known I loved him. The night before he broke my heart.

But, things had changed dramatically since then. I felt a happy gurgle in my stomach and a corny smile pull up on my face. Tor hadn't gone back to Shava. He'd come back for me.

I scouted the cave for food, suddenly famished. I found a box of soda crackers and a bottle of water and dug in.

I had no idea what time it was. I was even blurry on what day it was, and also how long Tor had been gone. I felt kind of groggy, so I stretched out on the cot and slept.

"Hey."

A tender shaking. Tor's beautiful face gradually came into focus.

"Sorry to wake you Dori, but it's time to go."

I sat up suddenly conscious of my ropy hair and soda cracker breath. "Did you get the bike?"

"Yes, and I brought you some of your clothes." He handed me a bag.

"You broke into my house?"

Tor smiled sheepishly. "It's not like the door was locked, and you have enough to explain without having to account for nakedness."

"True enough." I recognized the jeans, shirt and jacket. He'd also brought me underwear. I squirmed a bit when I pictured Tor scoping out my messy room and searching through my drawers. "Thanks."

After I changed, Tor walked me home.

Just before we got to my house I said, "You should go now."

"You're probably right. It wouldn't look good for you to have ridden off with one guy and be brought home by another."

I punched him playfully in the arm. "Are you going back to the cave?"

"I have things to check out for Uncle Dex."

"Will I see you in school tomorrow?"

Tor kissed me on the forehead. "I'll be there."

OF COURSE MY parents freaked out when I walked in the door. They went on a rant about how they didn't know me anymore, and why did I suddenly decide to get so rebellious. I gave them the story, trying to shift most of the blame onto Ky.

They finally calmed down after I reassured them I was all right, that Luke's bike was all right and that it was just an accident. We didn't mean to get lost. I was grounded for a month, only allowed out of the house for school and to walk Sidney. It was a punishment I readily accepted.

The first thing I did was wash my hair in the sink (thankfully, wet hair didn't turn me), and spray in tons of leave-in conditioner.

Then I texted Samara and Becca, telling them I was okay, got lost, etc, and would explain everything to them at school the next day.

Crosby ignored me, but Sidney sat on my rug panting expectantly.

"Mom," I said, easing down the steps, "I'm taking Sidney for a walk to the park."

Mom was peeling potatoes in the sink. I knew she was still peeved at me because she didn't turn around. "Come back right away, and I mean it."

"I will. I promise."

I jogged with Sidney; we both needed a good leg stretching. The park had more people in it than usual. A spot of sunshine drew them outdoors, opting to get what rays they could before winter set in.

A couple vacated a bench and I grabbed it. It felt weird not to have Ky here breathing down my neck. Weird in a good way.

I scrubbed Sidney's ears as he panted on my knee. I was about to head back when I saw a familiar form.

Colby strutted over, his fists in his pockets, his shoulders hunched.

"I thought I might find you here." He sat on the bench beside me.

"How did you know I was back?"

"Tor. He came by with my bike an hour ago."

Tor had been busy.

"He said that you were in trouble with Ky; that's why he needed my bike. Was it true?."

I groaned. "Yes. I feel so stupid now. Ky is bad news. I was an idiot to skip class with him."

"Well, you know I never liked the guy."

"I should've trusted your instincts."

Colby tapped his foot nervously. "So, you and Tor?"

Might as well rip off the bandage. "Yeah, we're back together."

"I thought so. I'm fine with it, just so you know."

"Really?"

"I mean I don't like it, but well, when you took off again this time, it just hit me. You're not the same girl you use to be. You're not the right girl for me."

I knew it wasn't fair for me to feel this way, but for some reason that hurt.

He continued, "I'm leaving in a couple years for university somewhere, hopefully on a scholarship..."

"Oh, I have no doubt, Colby."

"And, well, we'd be apart anyway. If we can't figure out how to do 'us' when we live in the same town, how could we ever do it long distance?"

I hung my head. Colby was a terrific guy. We would've been a great team.

"I wish things could've been different between us, I really do. But, I'm glad you're moving on. It's the right thing."

Colby's shoulders relaxed as he let out a long sigh. I reached with my hand and he leaned over. I rubbed his brush cut knowing that this was the last time I'd ever do it.

"You've been a good friend, Colby."

He stood up. "I should go."

I felt a lump in my throat. "Okay. See you tomorrow."

38

I found Samara and Becca at Becca's locker. Before I could even say 'hi' Samara bore her dark eyes at me. " 'Fess up, girl."

"I did something stupid."

Becca huffed, "No kidding."

"Ky talked me into cutting class. I don't know what made me do it. We took Luke's dirt bike."

"And you got lost?" Becca said this like she didn't believe it for a minute.

"Sort of. Becca, I know this is going to be hard for you to hear, but Ky is not a good guy, trust me. If it weren't for Tor..."

"Tor?" Samara said. "Wait a minute, is he back?"

"Yeah. Ky and I kind of ran into him and it gave me a chance to get away from Ky."

"So you didn't get lost with Ky?" Samara asked.

"Well, I did." At least figuratively. "But then I left with Tor and, uh, we got lost."

"But everyone's saying you got lost with Ky," Becca whined. "They're blaming him."

"I did get lost with Ky. He's the first one I got lost with."

Samara and Becca both looked at me like I was lucky or crazy.

"Anyway, Ky left."

Becca said, "What'd you mean?"

More story to weave. "He left with his family. They're cruisers, right? He always said he wasn't going to be around for long."

Thankfully, the bell rang before they could ask me any more questions, before I could paint myself further into a corner with half-truths.

Tor arrived at lunch time. I found him in the office registering for class. I pressed into him. "Hi."

He muttered into my ear, "You know I'm only putting myself through this again because of you, right?"

I laughed. "You won't be sorry." Or at least, I hoped not. You never knew around here anymore.

"Well, actually, I do want to get an education, so I suppose you're worth the trouble."

He was in my biology class now, instead of Ky, which suited me just fine. We walked the halls hand in hand. People seemed surprised to see Tor again, some of them giving shy waves or shouting out welcome back. Sawyer and Mike fist bumped him. Samara smiled knowingly, Becca begrudgingly. Tiffany just rolled her eyes.

I admitted to having a hard time concentrating on the lecture, knowing that it was Friday and this was all I would get of Tor until Monday morning.

He emailed me that night. He had their computer set up in the cave again. Tor said he had errands to run for Dex, so he wouldn't be moping around the cave all weekend. He ended his email with**…but I wish you were here.**

I wish I were there, too!

I wondered what kind of errands he was doing, and imagined it had something to do with tensions in the merfolk world. I smiled smugly when I pictured Prince Mol finding out we had escaped. I felt for the poor Lars who had to break that news.

The weekend went by blissfully uneventful. I slept most of Saturday and got caught up on my homework Saturday night.

Sunday morning my mom knocked on my door to announce that we were going to church.

"But we never go to church."

Mom sat on my bed. "Dori, when you went missing again, well, I just couldn't bear it. You don't know what it's like to be a mother and to worry about your children. It's like a rope in my whole being gets tugged every time I think of you and when I'm afraid for your life, this rope is pulled on so hard, I think it's going to snap.

"I got on my knees for you. And you're back. Safe and alive. So get up. We're going to church."

I was grounded so I couldn't argue, but it actually sounded like a good idea to me.

We went to a small protestant church, a wooden building with narrow siding that had been repainted several times—blue, yellow and now white. A narrow steeple above the solid double doors pointed to the sky. A simple iron cross sat on top.

I was surprised to see Nana there. So, Nana was going to church now, too? Mom slid into the pew beside her and I was kind of glad to have her body between us.

There was nice singing. A pastor read from the Bible and recited words of wisdom for us to apply to our lives. I zoned in and out a lot. I was still really tired, and I had a lot on my mind.

Afterward Nana asked Mom if she could take me for lunch. Mom hesitated and I sort of hoped she'd say no. I was grounded, right? But she agreed and left me standing in the square on Main Street alone with Nana.

"Come," she said. "Let's go to the Tea House."

The Tea House was a British style establishment which had pictures of the queen, and the royal kids hanging on the wall. A Union Jack flag was pinned up over the door, and the booths had vinyl seats in royal blue.

They served every kind of tea and the best scones that were simply to die for when you smothered them with Devonshire cream and raspberry jam.

I ordered Earl Gray and two fresh baked scones.

"Dori, honey, I know you've been upset with me, and I think I know why."

I didn't know what to say, so I took another bite of my scone.

"And I think I know where you've been these two times you've been missing. Shall we just be honest for once and get it all on the table?"

She took a sip of her tea and I did the same. "Yeah, Nana. I think it's time."

"I guess it's only fair that I start. I met Dex Riley when I was twenty, so a bit older than you are now. Benjamin–he was American, you remember, and was fighting in Vietnam at that time–and I had an understanding. Nothing official, we weren't engaged. He would be gone for months at a time. It's easy to drift apart when you don't see someone more than two or three times a year."

I'd seen pictures of Nana when she was younger. Her blond hair was long and wavy, not unlike mine. She had been pretty. She still was beautiful in a graceful, elderly way, and it didn't surprise me that she'd had men interested in her.

"I met Dex on the beach, much like I expect you met your friend?"

I nodded slightly.

"It started simply enough, just a friend, but after awhile, we both started to feel more. I'd decided early on that when Ben returned I would end it with him. I felt horrible, because I knew he was off fighting a terrible war and I was home having the time of my life. I couldn't help that I had fallen in love with Dex.

"One day Dex said he had something to tell me. His story was so wild, I couldn't believe it. Then he showed me. I dove into the water to be with him and I was wildly enamored. It was so fantastical and romantic.

"We had the most amazing summer. I spent every spare minute with him, either on land or swimming. It was a terrible chore to keep such a secret to myself, but who could I tell? You must know what I mean?"

I did.

"And as time went on, Dex had to return to the sea, sometimes for long stretches. I wondered where he went. He tried to explain things to me, what his family was like, how they lived, but I couldn't imagine it. I realized I would never be a part of Dex's other life.

"Then the war ended. I knew that Ben would be coming back to Maine and that he would want to make things official and get married. With Ben I could have a normal life, a husband who would stay home, children who could know both of us equally, and a comfortable community.

"Plus, I knew if I stayed with Dex there would be the possibility that our children could take after him, and I couldn't take that chance. So, I said goodbye to Dex and yes to Ben."

"You didn't know you were already expecting my mom?" I said.

Nana shook her head. "No. I've lived with this secret my whole life. What good would it have done to tell her the truth?"

"Besides, I never saw Dex again. I had no way of telling him. He didn't know about your mother, and Ben didn't know about Dex. And as you know, Ben and I never ended up having our own children. Your mother is the only one."

Nana took a sip of her tea and gazed out the window. The ocean waves capped and crashed onto the beach.

I'd judged Nana for what she did, but I understood now. If Ky hadn't come after me, Tor would've stayed away, and I would've chosen Colby even though I still loved Tor. Benjamin was Nana's Colby.

"I stopped going to church years ago because I believed that what I had done was unforgivable. Now I know that nothing is unforgivable. Things turned out they way they should have."

"I'm sorry, Nana, for being so hard on you."

"I'm sorry, too, dear. Now, are you going to tell me your story?"

I told her how I met Tor and what really happened that night at the bonfire. I explained how being around him had affected me physically and how Tor figured out I had merfolk blood in me.

"He's the one who told me about you, but I didn't find out about your connection to Dex until recently."

I told her about Crazy Jim hitting our sailboat and I got caught in his net, and how that if I hadn't been merfolk, I would've drowned that day. I went on to tell her about how I'd met the clan of Rai, and Tor's family. She laughed when I told her about Barnaculoese, and frowned when I told her why the Lars clan wanted me. I told her it was Crazy Jim who shot me when he saw my tail and how Tor had saved my life.

I told how I fell in love and had my heart broken.

It was difficult to tell her the parts about Ky and how I'd let him manipulate me, and how Tor had rescued me. Again. And then how it was my fault we were caught.

She scowled when I described Prince Mol and teared up when I told her that Dex had abdicated because of her.

"But it's fine now, Nana, he's king again."

"He never told me he was merfolk royalty."

"He is, and well, you know what that makes me?"

"What?"

"A princess."

"A princess?"

"Yes, the king is my grandfather. And I'm the sole heir. Well, the only one who can grow a tail."

Nana grew very quiet.

"You're not safe, here, Dori."

"I'm safer here, then there, and here is where I plan to stay for a long while."

"I'm glad to hear it. It's a lot to take in, isn't it?"

I agreed. We finished our meal in silence.

Nana put her arm around me as we walked home. It felt so good to be on her side again.

"Promise me something," she said when we reached my house. "Promise me you won't keep any secrets from me. You'll tell me if you decide to go back, for whatever reason?"

"I promise."

It was a promise I had to make good on before the night was out. I had an email waiting for me from Tor. The Lars had declared war.

or texted and said he would meet with me at "our rock" when I took Sidney for his walk. I smiled when I saw those words, *our rock*. I was glad to reclaim that landmark as a happy place.

The wind off the ocean could be chilly this time of year, so I chose a warmer coat and pulled a toque on my head. Sidney wagged his tail and yipped, overjoyed that we were finally headed to the beach again.

We crunched through the pebbly sand, staying well away from the water line. We climbed over the jagged rocks and Sidney barked like a mad dog.

"It's just Tor, Sidney. Chill."

He leaned up against the rock all stoic and handsome and a burst of warmth filled my chest.

I was about to run and throw my arms around him when I saw movement on the other side of the rock. A large, broad shouldered man.

"Dex?"

Last time I'd seen Dex, we we're both fashioning tails and I had thrown myself at him like a clingy fanatic. That was before I knew he was the king. That was before I knew he was my grandfather.

"Dori, please, come give an old man a hug."

I responded happily, "I don't know what to say. It's so good to see you!"

Dex held me back with his strong hands and stared at my face. "A granddaughter. I had no idea."

I held him tightly again. "I know. Isn't it crazy?"

I had Tor and I had my grandfather. I felt unbelievably happy. Until the bombshell.

"We have to leave tonight," Tor said.

"What?"

"The situation under the sea is very unstable. Uncle Dex wanted to leave early this morning, but I convinced him that we needed to see you first."

"He was right. I'm glad we came," Dex added. "I'd hate to think I didn't get a chance to see you...."

I felt panic squeezing my chest. "What's happening?"

"The Lars are encircling the seamounts. We expect they will attack within a couple days."

"But why do you have to go?" A desperate foreboding made me feel faint. "Aren't there enough other Rai to deal with this?"

Tor reached for my hand. "You know that they outnumber us. We need every man."

"And I'm their king," Dex said. "I have to be there to raise the morale."

"Well, don't you need every woman? I should go, too."

"No!" they both said, scaring me.

"Dori, dear," Dex began, "you must realize that it is of vital importance that the heir to the throne be kept out of danger."

"In case something happens to you?" I was incredulous.

"What would I do? I don't know how to rule a kingdom. Are you kidding me? Nothing can happen to you!"

"I didn't mean to frighten you, child. I'm sure I will be fine."

"And don't forget," Tor said. "Prince Mol still wants you."

I turned to him, beseeching. "Please, stay with me. I need your protection. You're both saying so." I felt so helpless and torn. I wanted Rai to fight and win. I just didn't want Tor and Dex fighting. I knew I was being selfish. All the Rai had loved ones who would fight. Not just me.

"You'll be fine here, Dori," Tor said. "And I'll come back, as soon as it's over, I promise."

I had to admit defeat. They were leaving and there was nothing I could do to stop them.

"How do you fight? What does a merfolk war look like anyway?"

Tor kicked the sand with his toe. "It's not very sophisticated, I'm afraid. The Lars clan use archaic weapons, whatever they can scavenge from ship wrecks. Mostly they are sneaky attackers. We don't have any real rules of engagement, since war between the clans has been so rare."

Dex rubbed his bushy eyebrows with his thumb and forefinger. "We, of course, can gain modern weaponry, but still fighting underwater is cumbersome. And we don't want to obliterate them unfairly, even if they are our enemy."

Like when Tor saved Crazy Jim, even though he had been attacking us. The Rai had a high ethical standard to maintain.

"Where is the battle?"

"The Lars are approaching Bear Seamount en mass."

"There must be something I can do," I said, a quiver in my voice. I could pretty much give up on remaining tearless. I wiped the first stray drop away with my fist.

Tor pulled me into a hug. "Just stay safe, Dori. That's what you can do."

Uncle Dex left Tor and me so we could say our goodbyes in private. I felt like one of those women you saw in history class saying goodbye to their men in uniform, hanky in hand, waving wildly at the trains as they chugged by.

I stewed the whole way home, sobbing quietly. Would I see them again? Wasn't there anything I could do?

Dad was in the living room when I got home, feet up on the recliner, jaw slack, sawing noises coming from his nose. He'd fallen asleep while watching the news. He was missing a story about a riot in some foreign city.

I watched with interest. It gave me an idea. I ran upstairs to see if I could do some wild on-line shopping.

40

———

A plan was formulating but I really had no idea if it would work. It could just make things worse. I had time to fret over it because even with rushed shipping, I had to wait for three days.

Samara and Becca didn't know what to do with me anymore.

"Where's Tor?" Samara asked on Monday when I met up with them in the hall. I needed a story that would make sense to them why Tor kept coming and going so much. I didn't have a good one yet.

"He's got the flu or something. Pretty bad. He'll be out for a couple days."

"That sucks."

"Well, I'm grounded anyway."

"Right." Mike appeared around the corner and Samara forgot all about me and my problems, taking Mike's hand and giggling as they strolled down the hall.

"They seem happy," I said to Becca.

She hugged her notebook to her chest. "Yeah, all these years they've been buddies, and who knew?"

I still sensed a thread of resentment.

"You know, Becca, it's not the end of the world if you don't have a boyfriend in high school. There's still all of college ahead of you."

"That's easy for you to say because you have a boyfriend. In fact, you've had your pick of boys."

No bitterness *there*.

"What's wrong with me anyway?" she whined.

"There is absolutely nothing wrong with you. It's all about timing and the right guy for you just doesn't happen to live in Eastcove. Do you really want to waste your time and energy on a guy just to break up because he's not the one? Believe me, *that* is no fun."

Becca sighed. "My mom says high school is for school. Guys are a distraction that keep you from getting good grades."

"Sounds like she's been talking to my mom. If she had her way, she'd ground me for life and I'd never have another boyfriend ever again."

Becca laughed. It was good to see her smile again. The bell rang and we each headed to our own class, but for the first time in a while I felt hopeful that our friendship could get back on course.

Outside of my constantly checking the mail and hoping for a delivery, the next three days were like old times. I hung out with my friends at school, walked Sidney afterwards, ate dinner with my family in the evening, and did my homework at night. Mom was in her glory and I hated that I was about to turn her world all upside down again.

I did do some investigating while I waited. I researched the co-ordinates of the seamounts, particularly Bear. I mapped out how to get there by boat and how long it would take. Longer than if I swam as a mermaid, but I promised Tor I'd stay safe. I had to keep dry. Or at least out of the water.

On one of my lunch breaks I went down to the harbor to see Harvey Smith at the boat rental place. I knew he had one novelty boat that he rented to tourists that had a glass bottom. Harvey didn't normally rent to minors, but I told him I was planning a surprise. He conceded because he knew me and I paid cash. Between the boat rental and my on-line purchases, all the money I made working over the summer had dried up fast.

On Thursday late afternoon I saw the UPS truck pull up. I ran outside before he could ring the bell and alert my family of the delivery. Two good size boxes. I hid them under the bushes.

I said goodbye to Mom on Friday morning, like I was on my way to school per usual, but instead of catching a ride in the Rotten Apple, I told Luke I felt like walking. Then I hiked over to Nana's.

She didn't answer when I knocked on the door, and I double checked the house but it was empty. I followed the well-worn path to the ocean.

Nana was there, sitting on a rock staring out to the sea.

"Nana?"

"Dori, honey, what are you doing here?"

"You told me never to keep secrets from you, so I have one I need to share."

Nana pursed her lips together like she knew she wasn't going to like what I had to say, but patted the rock beside her.

I sat and we watched the waves lick the shore, and shooed the seagulls away from our heads.

"I haven't seen him in almost forty years," she said, staring out at the horizon.

"He's seen you."

She jerked. "What do you mean?"

"I've seen him watching you. When you're shopping and hanging out on Main. I think he still loves you."

Her wrinkly hand covered her mouth. "Oh, my."

"That's why you come here all the time, isn't it? You're hoping to see him again."

Now she wrung her hands, staring into space. "It's been a childish fantasy of mine, I'll admit. And once Benjamin passed away, I really let my mind go. It's silly."

"It's not silly. It's sweet."

"Well, he hasn't tried to talk to me. I've been here all along."

"He's just honoring your request. The Rai are like that. If he knew you wanted to see him, he'd come. I know it."

She looked at me steadily, her gray eyes watering from the wind. "Will you tell him?"

I nodded. "Of course. But there is a reason I came to see you. The clans are fighting."

"Fighting?"

"Like, war. The Lars declared it."

"Oh no, that's terrible. But what does this have to do with you?"

"The Rai are out-numbered. The manner in which they are fighting is ineffective and outdated. And, Tor and Dex are in the battle."

Nana drew a sharp breath.

"So, I have a plan, but it means breaking my curfew."

Nana shook her head. "You're not going *in* are you?"

"That's not the plan, but I might be gone for a while. Nana, I think you should tell Mom the truth."

She blanched a bit at that. "I suppose it's time." She patted my knee. "Don't worry. I'll deal with your mother. You just go do what you have to do to save our men."

I wrapped my arms around her and she kissed my forehead. "I love you, Dori."

"I love you, too, Nana."

41

Imanaged to abscond with my packages without being noticed. It took a bit to balance both boxes as I walked to the harbor. At least they hid my face. I got the keys for the glass bottomed boat from Harvey.

He eyed my boxes.

"Supplies," I said. "For the surprise." Which wasn't entirely untrue. Tor was about to be surprised.

I hopped on board, set the coordinates and hoped the technology on the boat was accurate. The weather wasn't too bad for this time of year, a little choppy, but if all went well I should get to the seamounts before too long.

And I hoped I wasn't too late.

Behind me Eastcove became a small dot until it disappeared altogether. I kept driving east until I was unable to see any land at all. I'd never been this far out before, and especially not by myself. I felt a tickle of nervous apprehension. It was an odd feeling to be out in the middle of the ocean with no landmarks in sight, just three hundred and sixty degrees of water.

The signals on board told me I'd reached the surface area

above Bear Seamount. Though I thought I would've known without them just by the strange behavior of the wildlife. Pods of Atlantic dolphins, humpbacks and harbor seals skimmed along the surface in an outward fashion, like petals sprouting from the eye of a daisy. Obviously, there was something going on underneath that they didn't want to have any part of.

I cut the motor and dropped the anchor. Then I lay flat on the glass bottom. This was the part where I was hoping for a miracle. I was part merfolk. Could I see the merfolk world while in my fully human form?

I pressed my face to the glass. I could hear my pulse beating in my ears and my breath steamed up the surface making it harder to see. I wiped the glass clean with my sleeve.

Where are you? Why can't I see you? I strained my vision searching for flashes of red and blue, but I all I saw was a strangely empty sea.

Why couldn't I see? I flopped on my back, letting out a breath of frustration. I knew what I had to do, but I had to muster all my courage to do it. I had to, for Tor and Dex.

I took the bailing bucket and scooped it full of water. I removed my jacket and my sweatpants. Then I dumped the water on my head.

I lay on the glass floor, wincing through the tingling and stiffening of my legs as they transformed into a tail. It was itchy and tight and not nearly as smooth as when it happened while submerged.

I flipped onto my stomach, knowing I had little time before I converted back. I pressed my face to the glass and I let out a startled breath. A whole new underworld scene had developed. The Lars and the Rai were in the height of battle. Some had hand weapons but many just wrestled like frenzied sharks attacking each other.

I searched desperately for signs of Tor. His dark shaggy hair, the pattern of his tattoos.

Then I saw him. He was man to man with another familiar mop of hair. Ky Larson. I guess Tor hadn't killed him last time after all.

They had each other in a head hold, rolling and spinning through the currents. Their tails flipped manically as each of them tried to get the upper hand.

I sucked air.

A red ribbon floated away from their frenetic forms. Blood.

Pain tore through my torso. I yelled out scratching at the glass. This was the first time I had to go through this experience without Tor to comfort me. It was scary to be alone and consumed with so much pain.

I hugged myself hard, my nails biting into my forearms. *Breathe through it.* More pulling and tugging, each like a stabbing knife. I let out another yelp, then gradually the pain subsided. I waited until it was completely gone, and my breathing patterns were back to normal.

I was naked. With shaking hands I put my sweats back on. I lay on my stomach peering through the glass but I couldn't see the battle anymore. I just hoped that it wasn't Tor's blood I'd seen.

I opened the boxes. What I needed now was the bullhorn. I leaned over the edge of the boat, letting the rim of the bullhorn touch the water then shouted, "Tor!"

I kept shouting until finally, a dark head broke the surface.

I almost cried with relief.

"Dori! What are you doing here?"

I knew he'd be mad, but I hoped he'd at least listen. "Tor, I have an idea."

I tried to ignore the worry lines on his face or the deep

scratches on his shoulder. I showed him what I had in the second box and what I thought we should do.

"Hmm, it might work," he said thoughtfully. "And it won't hurt the other marine animals?"

"It won't hurt them, but it might make them uncomfortable. Whatever ones are still hanging around."

"Okay, it's worth a try. Give me thirty minutes to spread the word among the Rai warriors."

I had put on my waterproof watch that morning. It was the slowest moving thirty-minutes ever.

I rocked in the boat, tried to hum a song, imagined how Nana was going about telling my mom the truth about her birth and hoped that Mom was able to deal with it all. Not just that Grandpa Ben wasn't her biological father, but that she was part merfolk.

And that her daughter was a mermaid. I wondered how that'd go over. I figured we were both having a trying day.

Finally the thirty minutes passed. I took out the object in the second box. It was about the size of a bullhorn but heavier with a cylinder nose. It was a LRAD or a long range acoustic device. Also known as a sonic weapon.

Tor's job was to call all the Rai back into the caves. The Lars would misunderstand this as a victory for them, but it would be short lived. I wished I could see them, but I had to trust in their character that they would take a moment to congratulate each other and gloat. I bent over the edge, holding the bullhorn with my left hand and placing the nose of the LRAD into it with my right. When the bullhorn rim touched the water I pulled the LRAD trigger.

42

A long-range acoustic device was often used by riot police to control crowds, or by the military in battle, or by ships at sea to ward off pirates. The standard kind used in these situations were large disks that looked like drum heads whereas the one I'd used was more for wildlife control and I was happily amazed to find it online.

I counted on it having a harsher effect underwater. It worked by sounding intense ultrasonic blasts, a high frequency noise that was very uncomfortable and sometimes painful to hear. It also caused nausea and headaches. My hope was that it would break up the battle and drive the Lars away.

But did it work?

I considered a repeat of the head drenching so that I could look through the glass and see what was going on, but the thought of going through that painful transition again and without Tor made me tremble. I decided to give him some more time to find me.

The skies were painted with streaks of pink as the sun began to set. A deep grayness rose up from the horizon and I knew I had to get going soon if I was going to get back before dark.

I'd gotten so fidgety, with nothing to do on the boat but waiting and imagining the worst case scenario, I was tempted to jump in and find out what the deal was when Tor's head popped up.

"What took you so long?" I spouted.

"Dori," Tor's eyes were bright with giddiness. He ignored my question. "That was genius. You are a genius!"

It was. I was?

There was a wooden slat foot step that ran along the width of the boat at its stern. Tor pulled himself up onto it so his body pressed against the boat, but his tail stayed in the water. I leaned over and kissed him, long and steady. *I* helped fight this battle. Tor thought *I* was genius.

"So what happened?" I said pulling away slightly.

"It worked. The sonic blast completely disoriented them. They swam away like little children, hands over their ears. We could hear it, but it didn't affect us the same way in the caves."

Tor was beyond excited. "The best part is, they have no idea what it was, but they know we had a hand in it. Otherwise, why did we all suddenly disappear into the caves just before it went off? It's put us back into a position of power. Thanks to you!"

I felt like jumping up and down. This was fantastic.

"You need to go home now, Dori. It's getting dark."

"I know. I just had to wait to find out how it went. Are you coming?"

"Tomorrow. I'll meet up with you tomorrow."

I remembered Nana and her request. "Will Dex come?"

A slight shadow crossed Tor's face. My head spun. "Is Dex okay? He's not..."

"No, he's fine," Tor said quickly. "He's injured but not dead. He'll probably come, too."

"Tell him that Nana wants to see him."

Tor smiled with a smirk in the way you did when you think of geriatric romances. "He'll come for sure, then."

I returned the keys to Harvey just before closing.

"So were they surprised?"

"They sure were." I was still in a state of euphoria, and it was impossible for me to wipe the grin off my face.

I carried my two boxes home, leaving them outside to retrieve later. I had enough to explain to my parents without adding questions about why their daughter was in possession of a sonic weapon.

Mom sat in her chair in the living room. She hadn't turned the lights on as the room darkened. Her expression was flat and her eyes dull, looking blankly out the window. My earlier state of elation deflated like a slow leak.

"Is Nana here?"

"I sent her home."

"Are you okay?"

"I'm better now that you're back. But no, okay isn't a word I'd use to describe myself right now."

I wasn't a therapist. I had no idea what the right thing to do or say was, so I just sat in the dark and quiet with her.

"You skipped school again."

"I know, I'm sorry."

"Nana says you're a mermaid, that when you disappear it's because you're swimming in the sea with some boy."

Oh, Nana, why'd you have to bring Tor into it? No sense denying it though. I was about to admit it when Mom continued,. "I think your Nana needs to see a doctor."

Oh.

"Besides telling me that my daughter's a mermaid, she told me my father's not my real father. That some *merman* is."

"And you don't believe her?"

Mom scoffed. "Of course not! I'm worried, Dori. I have a rebellious daughter who no longer stays in school and a senile mother who wants to change the way I view my dead father."

I closed my eyes and groaned. I was the one who'd convinced Nana to tell Mom. Looks like I'd made a really bad call.

"I'm sure Nana's fine. She probably just had an off day. Or maybe she was just trying to distract you so you wouldn't worry so much about me."

Mom got out of her chair and walked over to me. She bent down and pushed a strand of fly away hair behind my ear. "I am worried about you. Why won't you talk to me?"

I wanted to, I really did. But if she didn't believe Nana, she wouldn't believe me. And I wasn't ready to prove anything to her yet.

43

It was unusually quiet in my house for a Saturday morning. Instead of kitchen noises and my mom busy whipping up some sort of food stuff, like canning fruit or baking bread, there was only the fridge hum and the ticking clock. Bright sunlight filtered stubbornly through the unopened blinds. Dirty dishes filled the sink and I felt a type of panic. Mom always left her kitchen spotless.

"Mom?"

I saw her profile when I peeked into the living room. She sat in the armchair, alone in the dark, just staring into space. I opened the curtains.

"Are you all right?" I asked.

She glanced up with heavy-lidded eyes and a blank face. I hated seeing her this way and longed for my happy, busy mother who annoyed me with her benign questions.

She shrugged. "I'm fine."

I didn't believe her, but my stomach was yelling and I needed breakfast before I could get into a heavy conversation.

Dad and Luke had gone into Saint John to check out a deal

on another sailboat (good thing the insurance on it included collision), so it was just the two of us in the house plus Sydney and Crosby. I made sure their food and water bowls were full before attempting to fill mine.

I shook an empty cereal box in Mom's direction. "We're out of Cheerios."

I made us both some toast, slathering the pieces with peanut butter and jam, and took her a plate, a type of peace offering.

"It's going to be okay," I said.

She nodded and made an effort to smile. I wondered if it would help if I jumped in the tub or something, to prove to her that Nana wasn't crazy and I wasn't trying to be rebellious. But, I had a feeling that scene might just push her over the edge. I'd have to ease her into the truth when I had more time.

I glanced at the clock. Thirty more minutes.

I busied myself by filling the dishwasher and wiping down the counters, and then I called Sidney for a walk.

"I won't be long," I told my mom as I left.

We headed for the beach, and Sidney ran ahead as I broke into a jog behind him. The only thing on my mind was Tor. He'd better be there, with legs on.

I wasn't disappointed. His green eyes lit up when he saw me.

"How's the day saver?" he said walking to me. "You wouldn't believe how famous you are now."

He gave me a long, savory kiss and I melted into him. The sea breeze blew around us, entangling our hair. The seagulls circled around, squawking and we could hear harbor seals barking in the distance. It was like nature was demonstrating her favor. I'd never felt more sure about my new life as a member of the Rai clan and with being together with Tor.

"Even more famous than before?" I said through our lips.

"Way more."

We moved back to our rock and Tor helped me up.

"I'm not sure you really understand what all of this means for you," he said after a moment.

"All what means?"

"You have a choice to make someday. You can take your rightful place as queen of Rai, once Uncle Dex steps down, that is, or...." He breathed in deeply. "You may want to live your life fully human on land. Somewhere far from the ocean."

"What? Those are my only choices? Why can't I just be Rai and not reign?"

"You could of course. So, I suppose you have three choices, but you are the heir. It is your destiny as Rai to rule one day."

Wow. This was too much. I hadn't even gotten used to the idea of being a princess, and to consider being more than that, to be queen, I just shook my head.

"Dex is going to be around a long time, so, it's not a decision I'll have to make any time soon."

"I don't know about that."

"What'd you mean?"

"Uncle Dex is visiting your grandmother as we speak. If she will have him, he's prepared to give up the throne again."

I felt faint. This was all happening too fast.

"But what about school? I can't just quit high school."

Tor leaned in closer. "No one's asking you to quit high school."

My head was spinning. "I don't know. I need to think about it."

Tor turned and pressed his forehead against mine. "Take as much time as you need."

"What happens if Dex wants to abdicate before I'm ready to... uh, step in?

"My father will reign temporarily until you're ready."

"If I'm queen one day," I whispered, "what will that make you?"

He kissed the tip of my nose. "Your servant."

I jolted back to stare at him. "Seriously?"

He laughed. "Well, yes and no. As queen, all the Rai are in your service. But we'd still be cousins."

"*Second* cousins."

He laughed. "Yes."

"So we could still date?"

He kissed my mouth while saying, "Definitely."

I thought of Nana and Dex and wondered how their reunion was going. And how Nana was going to break the news to my mom.

"Princess or almost queen or whatever, I'm still grounded," I said, tugging on Tor's hand as I hopped off the rock. "Do you mind if we hang out at my place today? I think my mom's going to need me."

The End

I hope you enjoyed reading *Seaweed*. Please help others enjoy it too.

Recommend it: Help others find the book by recommending it to friends, readers' groups, discussion boards and by suggesting it to your local library.

Review it: Please tell other readers why you liked this book by reviewing it at Amazon or Goodreads.

Discover the CLOCKWISE COLLECTION!

Almost sixteen-year-old Casey Donovan just wants to survive high school ~ uncontrollable trips to the 19th century do NOT help, especially when you accidentally take the cutest boy in the school back in time!

Buy on Amazon or read FREE with Kindle Unlimited!

Read on for the first chapter.

CLOCKWISE - CHAPTER ONE

EVERYONE HAS TO LIVE with something.

For instance, my hair is the unmanageable kind of curly, the color of burnt toast. Imagine waking up every morning looking like the Lion King, or having to spend a disproportionate amount of your allowance on hair products that don't deliver. Like the ones under my bathroom sink. Row after row of half-empty containers of mousse, gel, and hair tamer standing dejectedly like the third string of a basketball team that rarely gets to play.

The thing is, I would be fine with rag mop hair, truly, if only I didn't have this other issue: uncontrolled time travel to the nineteenth century. I've never met anyone else with the same problem, either, so that also classifies me as some kind of freak.

On the upside—like a blind girl who ultra develops her other senses to compensate for what she can't control—I've picked up a few extra skills along the way. One survival reflex I've nurtured is how to be quick on my feet. I have good impulses, you could say.

Well, normally, this is an upside.

Until a second ago.

I was sitting with my best friend, Lucinda, on the sidelines of the football field. As usual, we were watching the yummy football players, rather than the scrimmage going on because really, who cared about the actual game? Despite the glare of the setting sun, I saw the brown speck hurtling towards me.

Impulsively, I jumped up and thump, Nate Mackenzie's football, signed by the famed Tom Brady himself, was in my arms. I couldn't believe it. I'd caught Nate Mackenzie's ball!

Gingerly, I raised my head. Sauntering across the field, with all his hunky hotness, was the cutest boy in the school, the most valuable senior varsity football player of Cambridge High, and the love of my life. He stopped right in front of me.

"Good catch." His rugged and manly voice lassoed me. He'd said *good catch.* I couldn't move or take my eyes off his face. The way the sun glistened off his sweat, emphasizing his strong jaw and the brightness of his blue eyes, brighter still because of the contrast of his dark, shaggy hair...

"So, can I have my ball back?"

My hands gripped his football with sticky sweat. The ticker tape in my brain searched for the right response before flashing ERROR in red neon twelve-point font.

"Casey?" Lucinda nudged my back. With a slight swivel of my head I saw her expression. Mortification. *Give the dumb ball back!* Did I just have an aneurysm? I felt woozy, like throwing up. I imagined myself vomiting all over Nate's feet.

Unbelievably, there are some things worse than puking in front of the football team. A wave of dizziness threatened to wash me away into black nothingness. But I couldn't be so lucky to just faint. It was happening. Oh no. Not here. *Please, not in front of Nate Mackenzie.*

In an instant, my world brightened like a nuclear blast as I spiraled through a long white tunnel. When I opened my eyes, he was gone. Nate was gone and so were Lucinda and all of Nate's football team.

I stood alone, in the middle of a lush forest painted every shade of green. My lungs filled with the sweet scent of undamaged air, my skin tingled with warm humidity. The furry and feathered inhabitants squealed and chirped with enthusiasm. I heard an unwelcome whistling noise and a pop. Nate's ball, still in my hands, had an arrow sticking out of it.

So much for quick thinking and quick feet. I jumped behind a tree and hid as a couple of kids, maybe ten and twelve, cantered by on horseback.

"You missed it!" teased the older boy. The fortunate squirrel scurried up the tree, its little feet loosening bits of bark that rained down on my head. I could have been killed or at least drastically injured, but all I could think about was Nate's football. The air seeped out as I tugged on the hand-whittled arrow. I slid down the side of the tree and groaned.

Tom Brady's signature had a puncture hole right in the middle of it. I gripped the flattened ball as I stomped through the brush, pushing scratchy branches away from my face. *Why did this have to happen in front of Nate Mackenzie? Why?*

Pack your bags, self-pity. I was cursed with time traveling. I was a slave to it with no control over when or *in front of who* it happens, and as far as I knew there was no cure. Not that I had anyone to ask about it. I just had to survive, which fortunately, I'd gotten pretty good at.

I soon came to a wide dirt road scarred with uneven grooves ground in by irregular carriage travel and dotted with hazardous looking empty potholes. I imagined they filled up unattractively with muddy water when it rained. A waist-high rectangular stone marker, leaning slightly like a wounded soldier, had the miles to Cambridge MA etched in it. Good. I knew where I was.

Time travel, as expected, is fraught with complications. The immediate one is what to wear. Or more like what not to wear. As in blue jeans and sneakers I needed to ditch ASAP. I slipped back into the dense covering of the forest and kept hiking. The second immediate problem has to do with food and drink. Let's just say that to solve these problems, you have to get creative.

I recognized a thick grove of lilac bushes and pushed my way through to the center, where a patch of wild grass opened up like a bald spot on the top of an old man's thick crown of hair. When I travel—and this started when I was nine years old—I always end up in the same locale. The actual spot on the planet Earth stays the same; just what is on it is different. In the future, this is the location of my neighborhood.

I lifted off a thatch of twigs to expose a deep hole; one I had proudly dug myself having *borrowed* a shovel from a neighboring farm. Inside was a hatchet, spotty with rust, a piece of flint, a rugged slingshot and two musky smelling burlap bags, which I pulled out, one at a time. The first had food—dried beef, raisins and a jar of well water. I opened the jar, took a drink and grimaced. Stale. The second bag had clothing: a long ivory cotton dress with tiny bluebells hand stitched in a scattered pattern, ladies boots that looked like figure skates with the blades off, a pair of trousers, a pair of men's boots, (yes, my feet were big enough to wear men's) and a boy's cap. I'd *borrowed* these during various trips, and hoarded them away for the "future."

A stumpy, fallen log, green with moss and partially hollowed out by ants, served as a bench. I rested against it, laying Nate's ball on the ground. I stared at it hypnotically, until I was lulled into a deep daydream, back to the football field at Cambridge High. This time I did everything right.

Nate says, *Good catch*, his eyes admiring me and my obvious, though previously hidden, athletic ability. I say, *Thanks*, and smile back with confidence, my hair perfectly tamed and my jeans fitting me exceptionally well. And most importantly, I give the ball back, offering it like a prize, our fingers lightly brushing in the pass. Nate throws it far and long, glancing back to see if I am still watching him.

I screamed. A garter snake had slithered over my hand. I jumped to my feet and did a little impromptu rain dance. I wasn't even afraid of garter snakes, it just startled me. My heart settled back to normal speed and I shook my head, trying to clear it. *Focus, Casey.* Sometimes it was difficult separating my two crazy worlds. I so didn't feel like being here in my alternate universe, the year 1860.

I put on the trousers. Fortunately, the fashion for boys in the nineteenth century was loose and baggy, so no need to lie flat on my back to wrestle with a zipper (which wasn't invented yet, anyway). Picking up Nate's ball, I tucked it securely under my shirt. I had to make sure the ball came home with me when I went. It served a second useful purpose, adding the illusion of boyish thickness to my waistline. A bit of twine made for a functional belt.

Shoot. The pant legs ended at my ankles. Okay, I forgot to add to my list of imperfections, (chronic bad hair days, the time travel thing, paralyzing crush on a way unobtainable hottie) that I'm also overly tall. Not graceful catwalk model tall or academy award winner beauty tall. More like ostrich tall. Without the feathers. Long limbs with knobby knees and elbows.

I pushed my hair behind my ears and into the cap. I hadn't picked up the habit of wearing make-up because a) a bare face aided me in my attempts to blend in and b) it was a liability to me when I traveled and wanted to pass myself off as a boy. I practiced at lowering my voice: Hello, my name is Casey.

I cleaned up my stash and worked to wipe out the evidence of a human visitation. I decided to head for the Watson farm, to see if Willie Watson would hire me again. It was grunt work, cows and chickens and the like, but it gave me a way to make a bit of money and get food. There were also a ton of kids and I could easily get lost in the mix.

At the main road I turned east towards Boston. Mid autumn leaves shook in the cool breeze causing goose bumps to pop up on my arms in defense of the chill. I rubbed them vigorously with my long fingers. Behind me I heard the growing rhythmic clip-clop of a single horse and cart. A young man with a mass of red, curly hair came to a stop at my side, stirring up a minor cloud of dust. I recognized him despite that fact he had filled out since the last time I'd seen him and unfamiliar stubble now shadowed his face. It was Willie Watson.

"Can I offer you a lift?" he said.

It was show time. I lowered my voice. "Willie?"

"Casey?"

"Yeah, it's me."

He cupped his hands over his eyes to block the sun. "I hardly recognized you. You've gotten so tall."

"I've heard."

"Where you off to?"

I shifted my weight, in a manly (I hoped) way. "Well actually, I was wondering if I could work for you again."

Willie nodded. "We can always use an extra hand. Get in."

I shared the back of the cart with a bale of hay and a little goat with a gray beard. Willie snapped the reins, the initial thrust tossing me to the back end of the cart where I settled in for the ride. I was happy to get out of the long walk to the

Watsons' farm, not too happy about hitching a ride with a goat. It sensed my discomfort and immediately reached over to nibble on my shirt. I swatted the air between us. "Back off!"

Willie called over his shoulder. "What happened to you? You just took off last time without saying anything."

I had my cover story ready. "I had to get back to Springfield. Family stuff. But my ma just had number thirteen so Pa sent me out to work again."

"Aye, I understand. My own mother is kept to her room with number ten."

I'd first met Willie when we were both twelve. He'd caught me stealing eggs from their chicken coop. Not my finest moment, I admit, but I plead desperation, driven to petty theft due to the fact that I had crossed off day eight in the past. Up until then, my trips had usually only lasted a couple days, but that summer things changed. Hungry and panicked, I'd thought I was stuck in the past forever, never to return home, never to see my parents or my younger brother, Timothy, ever again. I'd crept like a fox at dawn to the nearest farm.

Thankfully, that was the Watson farm, and the Watsons had turned out to be the nicest and kindest people I'd ever met. Anyway, Willie had caught me with my hand in the cookie jar, so to speak. "You gonna eat those raw?" he'd said. I hadn't thought about that. I'd shrugged, too stunned and frightened to say anything of intelligence. "We have hotcakes in the kitchen, you can come for breakfast." The thought of eating with all those Watsons was just too scary. My face must've reflected that, since Willie went on to say, "That's okay, I'll bring you some. Wait for me on the dock." I'd nodded and watched in silence as Willie gathered the eggs before leaving.

I'd made my way to the small lake situated in the middle of the Watson farm, thinking that I was either going to get a yummy breakfast or Willie was going to return with a gun and take me to the jail house. He'd showed up with breakfast.

"Thanks," I'd said. Willie's voice hadn't yet changed so he didn't think twice about my high-pitched squeakiness. I ate the warm and sticky pancakes with my dirty, bare hands. I'd tried to imagine what I looked like to Willie. I hadn't showered in ten days, and my hair was grimy and in hysterics. Just like those kids in Lord of the Flies after a few weeks without parents to boss them around. He never snitched on me about my chicken house raid and got me a job pitching hay. I'd stayed in the past for a full three weeks, and from that point on the "rules" of time travel had altered. Now, I never knew how long I'd be gone.

We rode the rest of the way to the farm in silence. Well, except for the goat, ba-aa-ing and nipping at my pant legs.

I rubbed my butt when we arrived, though the bumpy ride was appreciated by both me and the goat.

"I could use help milking the cows and keeping the barn clean," Willie said, pointing to the prominent red out-building behind the stately family home. "You can sleep in the loft, like last time," he added. I strutted away, concentrating on my gait, mimicking my brother's boyish walk. Swiveling hips would get me into big trouble. Times like this made me thankful for my poached egg sized breasts. Just call me *Mr.* Casey.

Someone watched me walk across the yard. Of course, there were plenty of people around, other workers, Watson kids playing tag, but I felt his eyes on me. Cobbs. He was shorter than me now, but beefy like a boxer with a round beer belly popping out. His face was pink and shiny and his dark beady eyes scanned my body.

Ew, what a perv. *I'm a boy, weirdo!* Or could he tell I wasn't? Did he remember me from before? Either way he was a creeper. I let my gaze fall to the ground and kept walking, away from the barn. When I was sure Cobbs was out of sight I circled back and slipped into the barn, climbing the ladder to the loft. I hid in the pokey straw and even though it was only dusk, I immediately fell asleep.

The tiny irritating saw of a mosquito buzzed near my face, and I flapped my hands dramatically. A rooster crowed and I sighed, disappointed I was still in the past. Not that I would travel in the night. I never traveled while sleeping. Ever. Didn't know why. Some kind of time travel law.

And I was hungry. Better go milk me some cows and earn my breakfast. A dozen Jersey cows lined up in a row. Grabbing a tin pail and wooden stool, I settled in under Betsy One. I called them all Betsy: Betsy One through Thirteen.

Willie joined me. "Mornin', Casey." He grabbed a short three-legged stool like the one I sat on, and plopped a pail under Betsy Three. It had been a while since I'd had to milk a cow, and honestly, I never did get the hang of it. First of all, cow teats are like short slippery ropes. Kind of gross to touch. And you have to pull on them just so, sort of a milk-releasing-rhythm. The cows get fully irritated when you don't get it right.

Thwap, thwap, thwap. The sound of milk shooting into a metal pail. Unfortunately, not my pail. Willie was showing me up.

I peeked around the back end of Betsy One, spying on Willie's Olympic cow milking performance. Betsy One didn't like my peering around her rear end, and whacked me hard with her tail. Kind of like getting smacked with a bull whip, but one covered in fur.

"Ouch!"

"You okay, Casey?" Willie called.

"Uh, yeah, fine." I mimicked Willie's timing, one, two, three, four, and thankfully the milk started to shoot out.

By the time I finished my fifth cow, (meaning Willie

whipped my butt by milking eight), my forearms burned and throbbed like mad. We carried the pails to the kitchen where the Watson kids poured the milk into jars so the older boys could make deliveries in the neighborhood.

The eldest Watson kid, Sara, oversaw the whole operation. Her red hair was parted down the center and two braids close to her face looped up like crimson handles. Though fashionable for this century, not a very becoming look as far as I was concerned. It seemed like she had a large lampshade under her skirt, the way it spread out at the bottom, and since women didn't normally wear hoops while working at home, I assumed that she must be about to go out. When she saw me, she propped her hands upon her waist.

"Willie," she called. "Who do we have here?" She didn't remember me because Willie, and his father when he was around, took responsibility for farm staff. She, when her mother was ill or with child, controlled the kitchen and house staff.

"Ah, you remember Casey Donovan? He's worked here before."

"Really? I don't recall." Sara pinched her eyebrows together. Then she called out, "Duncan, Josephine, Charlotte, Abigail, Jonathon!" A collection of kids with either curly red or brunette hair entered the room.

With the guidance of a stout and bright faced woman named Missy, they went to work bottling the milk, careful not to get knocked to the ground by Sara's hoop skirt.

Willie left and I turned to follow, but she cleared her throat, stopping me. I waited to be dismissed, but she held my gaze. She got right to the point. "How old are you?"

"Uh, almost sixteen."

"Do you shave, Casey?"

"Uh," My hand jumped to my chin. "Sometimes. I'm a late bloomer. It runs in my family."

"I dare say. Did you spend the night in the loft?"

"Yes."

"Alone?"

"I think so. I fell asleep shortly after my arrival yesterday. I don't remember seeing anyone else."

"That's a relief," she said.

"Why is that?"

She removed her apron and smoothed out her skirt. Then she looked me straight in the eye. "Because Casey Donovan, I believe that you are a girl as surely as I am one."

Buy on Amazon or read FREE with Kindle Unlimited!

ABOUT THE AUTHOR

Lee Strauss is a USA TODAY bestselling author of several cozy historical mystery series and young adult books including; The Clockwise Collection (YA time travel romance); The Perception series (young adult dystopian); Seaweed; and Love, Tink; with over a million books read. She has titles published in German, Spanish and Korean, and a growing audio library.

When Lee's not writing or reading she likes to cycle, hike, and stare at the ocean.

leestraussbooks.com

ACKNOWLEDGMENTS

Special thanks to Nathan Van Zyderveld for insights on sailing and to Lori Van Zyderveld for her heartfelt moral support and mad proofreading skills!

Thanks eternally goes to my family and friends who continually cheer me on from the sidelines (I'm looking at you, Marie Clarke <3) and to God who has blessed me with the best job evah!